THE ROOKIE

KIMBERLY KINCAID

THE ROOKIE

DEDICATION

This book is dedicated to
Avery Flynn and Tracey Livesay
who encouraged me to "write what you want!"
This book of my heart would not
exist without your advice.
And that is totally not the margaritas talking.
Mostly.

1

As far as Tara Kingston was concerned, not all murderers were created equal. Some killed people out of hate, some out of anger or revenge. Some were twisted enough to do it for chuckles. Some—and this category had always had the ability to chill Tara's skin and send her stomach toward her Manolos—were frightening enough to do it for no reason at all. The murders Tara had helped to prosecute in her three years working in the Remington District Attorney's office had ranged from emotion-fueled snap decisions to calculation and ice-cold blood. There was only one thing that every single one of them had in common.

The people who'd committed them all deserved to pay for their crimes. And even though it wouldn't reverse the one senseless murder that mattered to her most, Tara could make sure that when wrong was done, justice was served.

Because she was going to miss her best friend for the rest of her life.

"Stop," she said, her voice echoing through her office. The rest of the staff, including her workaholic boss, Bennett

Alvarez, were long gone. If she'd clocked enough hours to have even a hint of a weak moment, it was time to toss in the towel for the night. No one wanted a soft, sentimental lawyer —especially not the families of the victims of the case she was working on right now. Ricky Sansone had committed three murders, maybe more, while he was selling illegal guns and God only knew what else to criminals with rap sheets as long as Tara's leg. She'd busted her ass to work the case with Remington's Intelligence Unit, carefully cultivating an agreement with a young woman who worked in Sansone's nightclub to get her to work as an informant and testify against him. Between the intel they got from Amour—whose real name was Aimee and who wasn't even old enough to drink, let alone work in a seedy-ass nightclub that was really a front for Sansone's shifty extra-curriculars—and the evidence collected by the detectives at the Thirty-Third, Tara had been able to build a case and get an arrest warrant. Bail had been set at a staggering one million dollars, which Tara had thought was a victory...right up until Sansone had posted it.

But his days breathing free air were numbered. He was dangerous. *Deadly.* She was going to need all the fortitude she could work up in order to prepare for the trial, but she would put him away forever.

Tomorrow, her weary brain told her, and her burning eyes ganged up in agreement. Thanks to the precautionary measures she'd insisted upon as a condition of his bail, Sansone was being carefully monitored by the RPD. Tara had six weeks until the trial started, and it was—shit—nine thirty on a Friday night. Her yoga pants and the leftover Pad Thai in her fridge were calling her name. She'd start fresh in the morning.

Turning in her desk chair, she powered down her laptop

and slid it into her bag. A few files went on top, along with the legal pad she'd jotted a few notes on throughout the day. Remembering the self-defense class she'd taken last year, Tara pulled out her keys so she wouldn't have to hunt for them in the dark and made her way out of her office, the sound of her heels clicking on the polished floor seeming overly loud with everyone gone. Exhaustion set in, turning her shoulders heavy as she stepped into the elevator, and she allowed herself the luxury of a too-long blink as the car descended to the ground level. The quick refresher gave her enough energy to steel her spine once the doors trundled open, and her legs took the autopilot route out of the building.

The night air was still residually warm from the brutal late-June heat wave that had put a chokehold on most of North Carolina over the last few days. Tara savored her inhale despite its muggy state, tucking back a strand of hair that had escaped from the twist at her nape. She needed to schedule a yoga class—she'd already missed two this week because of all this trial prep—and make sure she hit the dry cleaners tomorrow to pick up her lucky suit to wear in court on Tuesday. And, oh, she had to order flowers for her mom's birthday next—

The chime of her cell phone interrupted both her thoughts and the quiet, making her jump, then making her laugh at herself for doing so. Slipping her hand into the side pocket of her messenger bag, she palmed her phone and smiled at the name on the caller ID.

"Hi, Amour." Tara hit the button on the key fob in her other hand, shifting the phone between her shoulder and her ear as the locks on her BMW disengaged with a *beep-click*. "How's it—"

The pain-laced moan filtering over the line cut Tara's question off at the knees.

"Amour?" Dread shuddered down Tara's spine, cold and clammy despite the humid night. *Oh, God.* "Amour, talk to me. Where are you?"

"Tara," came the barely-there whisper.

"I'm here," she promised. "Tell me what's going on. Are you hurt?"

Amour's whimper in reply was all the affirmative Tara needed, the sound claiming her gut in an instant. "Please. Help me."

Tara's brain kicked her thoughts into action. "Don't hang up, do you hear me?" She flung her car door open, dumping her bag inside and yanking herself into the driver's seat. She needed to get EMS on the line so they could access the GPS in Amour's phone and send help. "I'm going to put you on hold and get nine-one-one on the line. Do *not* hang up, Amour."

Willing her fingers not to shake so hard they couldn't function, Tara pressed the *mute* button for three seconds that might as well have been a month, then dialed nine-one-one.

"Nine-one-one, what's your emergency?" the operator asked, his voice smooth and sure.

Tara's was neither. "My name is Tara Kingston, and I'm an ADA in Bennett Alvarez's office. I've got an informant on the other line who's in danger. I'm patching her through."

Praying that Amour was still there—*please, please, please* —Tara punched the button that would—*please*—bring her back on the line. "Amour? Are you there? There's an operator listening."

"Tara," she croaked. "It hurts."

"Ma'am, can you tell me where you are so I can send help?" the operator asked.

Amour whimpered. "H-home."

"Twelve Broadmoor Street, in North Point," Tara supplied, switching the call over to her car's Bluetooth and pulling out of her parking spot. She'd arranged for at least a dozen Ubers to take Amour home as they'd put together the case against Sansone. Of course, she was all the way across town, and *damn* it! Tara had to hurry.

"Ma'am, can you tell me if you're in danger right now?" The operator was trained to keep his tone calm, Tara knew, but the concern in his voice was obvious.

"I don't...know. There was a man," Amour murmured. "He...I can't...my...my head feels funny. Hurts."

Tara bit her bottom lip hard enough to make it throb, letting the nine-one-one operator do his job even though she wanted nothing more than to loosen the scream in her throat.

"I'm dispatching police and EMS to your location, ma'am," the operator said. "Do you know if the man is still there? Are you in danger?"

"I don't...see him...he...said...not to..." Amour's whisper faded into a white-noise *whoosh* of silence on the line.

Tara's heart vaulted against her breastbone. "Amour? Are you there?"

"Ma'am?" The operator's voice tightened. "Ma'am, if you can hear me, stay on the line. Don't hang up, even if you can't talk. Help is on the way."

Please, God, Tara thought as she jammed her foot even harder over the BMW's accelerator. *Please don't let me be too late again.*

～

"YOU TRY and lay claim to that Cuban sandwich, and me and you are gonna have words, rookie."

Xander Matthews looked up from the takeout bag in his lap and placed a hand over the Kevlar turning his patrol uniform into a sauna. This heat wave gave zero fucks about the fact that the sun had set, or that the air conditioning in the cruiser where he'd spent the last eleven hours was iffy, at best. Still, the smile he leveled at his partner was genuine.

"After all this quality time we've spent together, you think I'd do that to you? I'm wounded, Sergeant Dade. Truly."

She snorted, just as Xander knew she would. Despite her petite stature and her sweet, Halle-Berry looks, Lucinda Dade had a mile-wide reputation for being one of Remington's toughest patrol cops. But after a year of working a beat under her supervision, Xander also knew that she was as fair as she was fierce.

Also, a sucker for a good Cuban sandwich.

"Your charm's no good over here, Matthews," Dade said, her mouth forming a scowl that the rest of her expression couldn't make stick.

"If I'm charming, it's only because I learned from the best," Xander pointed out with a grin as he passed over her sandwich. While he might've been laying the rest on with a trowel just to mess with her—he was her partner, after all, which made him practically duty-bound to give her at least a *little* crap on occasion, rookie or not—the part about her being the best, he meant. Dade had served the Remington Police Department for fifteen years. She'd passed up numerous well-earned promotions to stay right where she was, preferring to "keep one eye on the street and the other one on rookies"—something she reminded him of at least daily.

Not that Xander minded. He was here to be a good cop, and that meant learning from the sharpest and most street-wise. If it also meant crazy hours (it did) and work hard enough to make most grown people weep (yep again), then so be it.

He was all too happy to keep his head down, his ears open, and his boots on the straight and narrow.

It was the least he could do to atone for the sins of his past.

"Mmm." Dade slid some PhD-level side-eye across the front seat of their cruiser before softening into a smile. "I am pretty damn good. And *you're* pretty damn lucky the guy running your sister's kitchen makes the best Cuban sandwich in the city."

"You're not going to get any arguments out of me on that one," Xander agreed. Kennedy managed one of Remington's most popular bar and grills, and she never hesitated to have a grab-and-go meal ready for him and Dade when they were on patrol. She hadn't been thrilled about his decision to become a cop—ever since they'd been reunited two years ago, she'd done some *serious* leveling up in the protective older sister department. Considering the dangerous circumstances that had brought them back together after five years of near radio silence, he couldn't exactly blame her. But Xander had been adamant.

He'd been a party to that danger, and a lot of really good cops had helped him out of a shit situation. Becoming a really good cop in return so he could help people, too? Made sense, no matter how dangerous it might get.

Before Xander could unearth the Tex-Mex turkey sandwich Kennedy had put in the bag for him—that homemade Chipotle mayo was a work of freaking art—the radio on the cruiser's dashboard crackled to life.

"Thirteen sixty-two, this is Main."

Dade's dark brows lifted toward her hairline in a non-verbal "not-it" as she held up her sandwich, which was already missing a sizeable bite.

Xander shook his head and scooped up the radio with a chuckle. "Main, this is thirteen sixty-two. Go ahead."

"Be advised, a nine-one-one caller is reporting a ten thirty-nine at twelve Broadmoor Street," came the report, and shit. Assault calls were some of the worst. *"Victim is non-responsive, unclear if suspect is still on-scene. EMS has been dispatched to the location and advised to wait for police assistance, over."*

Xander flashed Dade a look, but she was already nodding. Between her ridiculous driving skills and the fact that Xander knew North Point's streets as well as he knew the goddamned alphabet—maybe better—they could be on-scene in five minutes. Plus, someone was in trouble. End of shift or not, they needed to take this. "Main, this is thirteen sixty-two. We are responding to twelve Broadmoor Street, over."

"It's a damn sin to let this sandwich get cold," Dade muttered, hastily wrapping up her dinner and handing it back to Xander as she reached for her seatbelt. While most people would find her gripe a bit callous, given that someone had just been assaulted to the point of non-response, Xander knew better. Defense mechanisms were as much a part of keeping cops safe as good training and body armor. Dade focusing on her sandwich meant she *wasn't* focused on her adrenaline.

And that helped Xander not focus on his. "I could always drive if you want to eat on the way there," he offered sweetly, tugging his own seatbelt into place as Dade kicked the cruiser into gear and pulled away from the side street where they'd stopped to eat. He'd learned pretty damned fast that her sarcasm was the main ingredient in the defenses that kept her safe, just as his laid-back demeanor was his. It was a weird partnering that shouldn't work, and yet...

"Stop being cute," she warned.

A smile touched his mouth. "Yes, ma'am."

"I mean it, Matthews."

"Copy that," he said, his smile refusing to budge. The banter calmed him in its odd way, leaving him clear-headed enough to scan the quickly passing streets. The city wore its usual Friday night crowds, but luckily, most people deferred to the flashing red and blue lights on the cruiser. Xander measured both his breaths and his heartbeats in time with protocol. *Inhale*, survey the entire scene upon arrival for potential threats. *Thump-thump*, clear the scene so paramedics can administer first aid to the victim. *Exhale*, take statements. Canvas the area. Search.

Do whatever it takes to help the person who needs it.

Each neighborhood grew shabbier than its predecessor as they went deeper into North Point. Xander's pulse always worked differently up here, as if the neighborhood that had given him the rough edges he'd tried so hard to sand down could see right fucking through him. Sure, he'd gotten out. Lived in a nice apartment. Had a good job. Food in his fridge. An eighty-year-old neighbor who checked on him as much as he checked on her, because that's what people did downtown.

And after two years, North Point only needed two seconds to make him feel like an imposter.

"Okay," Xander said, dumping himself out of his thoughts and into the right-now of Broadmoor Street. "The house should be right up here, on the left." He slanted a gaze over everything the cruiser's over-bright headlights touched. "I don't see anyone." After a glance in the side-view mirror, he added, "But it looks like the ambo's right behind us."

"Copy that," Dade said. "Keep your head on a swivel."

"Always," Xander promised.

Putting the cruiser in *Park* in front of the nondescript single-story house, Dade radioed in their arrival, then got out of the car. Xander moved in tandem with her, both of them treating the scene to one last heavy visual before turning toward the ambulance that had pulled to a stop at the curb.

"Hey, Xander," came a familiar voice from the driver's side of the ambo. Cops and firefighters were like peas and carrots around the Thirty-Third, and EMS totally counted. Quinn Slater leaned through the open window, her husband/paramedic partner, Luke, sitting right beside her. "You want us to hang back?"

"For a minute, yeah. We'll move as fast as we can to secure the scene."

Dade tilted her head toward the house to indicate that this wasn't a tea party, and right. Time to go.

He fell into step beside her, his heart striking a brisk rhythm against his ribs as they approached the front door. The house was quiet, the single porch light casting a dingy glow over the worn boards, the flimsy screen door, and—

"Door," Dade murmured. Her hand moved to her weapon at the sight of the splintered front door jamb and the sliver of light spilling onto the porch from the interior of the house.

Xander didn't have time to register the knock-knock/who's-there between his adrenal glands and his pulse. At Dade's nod, he shouldered his way over the threshold, his own weapon drawn and all five senses on full alert.

The house was small enough for them to clear it quickly—just one front room, a kitchen, and a small dining area. Dade lifted her chin at the short hallway, which presumably led to a bedroom, and Xander metered the tightness in his lungs with a nod in reply. She led the way into the lone room in the corridor, moving soundlessly to the door on the far side of the room as Xander took the opposite side. Searching the tiny closet behind him took seconds, and he moved to the far side of the bed to clear the space.

Only a woman lay unconscious on the narrow stretch of carpet, a small but very real pool of blood beneath a wound at her temple, and Xander's body moved before his brain even realized the command to do so.

"Woman down," he said, at the same time Dade said, "Clear." Holstering his weapon, he yanked the pair of nitrile gloves he always had in his pocket over both hands, then knelt carefully beside the victim.

His exhale came fast and hard. "She has a pulse."

Relief flickered through Dade's dark eyes for the briefest of seconds before she reached for the radio on her shoulder to give Quinn and Luke the all clear. Xander stabilized the victim by cradling her head in his palms, trying not to let his gaze linger on the jagged gash spanning from her temple all the way into her matted blond hair.

She stirred at the contact, her eyes flying wide a half-second later.

"Whoa, okay, it's okay," Xander said in a rush. "My name is Xander Matthews, and I'm a police officer. I'm here to help you."

"He said...he was here, and he said..." Her voice trembled with raw fear, her body following suit beneath Xander's hands, but nope. Not today.

He parked himself directly in her line of vision, holding

her glassy eye contact with his own steadier stare. "I've got you, now. No one's going to hurt you."

The woman blinked, her body relaxing after a beat. Quinn and Luke crossed the threshold into the tiny bedroom less than five seconds later, working briskly to complete the Rapid Trauma Assessment that deemed a C-collar, backboard, and an immediate trip to Remington Mem necessary.

"On my count. One, two, three," Luke said, lifting the backboard in perfect tandem with Quinn and moving it to the gurney they'd had to leave in the hallway for the sake of space. All the better, really, since this place was clearly a crime scene.

Speaking of which…

"We're going to need to figure out what happened here," Xander said to Dade, who nodded her agreement as they followed about ten paces behind Quinn and Luke, heading back out into the muggy night.

"I'll call it in. One of us should—"

Her words cut short at the sight of a redhead in a skirt and blouse that looked like they cost the rough equivalent of Xander's monthly rent, beelining directly toward the ambo.

"Amour! Oh, my God. Are you okay? Is she okay?"

The sound of the woman's voice sailed straight past Xander's Kevlar and into his chest. No way. No fucking way. It couldn't be.

Quinn stepped in to intercept the woman before she could get too close. "Ma'am, I need you to calm down and take a step back, please."

"No, I will *not* calm down, and I sure as hell won't step back," she said, hands planted against her pinup-model hips as she glared at Quinn, and God damn it.

Tara Kingston was in the middle of his crime scene.

2

Adrenaline replaced the fear that had taken up residence in Tara's chest the second she'd seen all the flashing lights in front of Amour's house. But at least the buzz of energy taking a swipe at her composure right now was familiar territory—occupational hazard of arguing with people for a living—and as nice as the paramedic standing in front of her seemed to be, the woman was entirely misguided if she thought Tara was going to sit idly by.

"Tara Kingston, DA's office," she clipped out. Oh, God, Amour looked so frail and helpless strapped to that gurney, her head bundled in a pile of blood-tinged gauze. That bastard Sansone had to be behind this. "She's a CI," Tara added, much more quietly, because she couldn't be too careful. Or, apparently, careful enough. "One of mine."

The paramedic—Q. Slater, according to the name stitched over the RFD logo on her shirt—flicked a heartbeat's worth of a glance over Tara's shoulder before saying, "Okay, but she's got a head injury and we need to get her to Mem. Quickly."

Tara's fear made a comeback tour, tightening her rib cage beneath her slate gray blouse.

"I'm going with you."

"Sorry, but it's family only for transport," the other paramedic, a guy with light brown skin and a serious voice that brooked no argument—not even from adrenaline-soaked attorneys—said quietly. "Plus, we need to keep her stable, which means we need room to work."

Wait, how had he opened the back of the ambulance so fast? "You don't understand," Tara tried again as they collapsed the gurney's wheels with a hard *clack*. "She called me. Instead of nine-one-one, she called *me*. She doesn't have anyone else she can trust."

The female paramedic paused. "You can follow us to Mem if you want."

"Actually, she can't."

The male voice coming from behind Tara made her pulse stutter as she turned toward its source of origin. But the police officer standing in front of her didn't make sense. That voice, somehow both rough around the edges and quiet all at once, belonged to someone the DA's office had considered prosecuting. Someone she'd initially pushed to pursue. Granted, it had been two years ago, but the case had been pretty unforgettable. Arson. Fraud. Murder.

And Xander Matthews had been smack dab in the middle of the whole thing...

Right up until he'd broken the whole case wide open and helped the Intelligence Unit catch a killer.

"Xander? What are you doing here?" Tara blurted, her cheeks instantly heating at her lack of decorum.

"It's nice to see you, too, Ms. Kingston." The muscle that pulled across Xander's unfairly chiseled jawline translated the words into a lie, but Tara didn't have the time or inclination to apologize for her iffy brain-to-mouth filter before he continued. "I'm here because it's my job. And if you have any information on this assault, I'm going to need you to stay here to make a statement."

"No."

"Pardon me?"

Okay, so that might've come out a liiiiiittle bit strong. But —no, no, no—the paramedics already had Amour in the back of the ambulance and were less than two minutes away from getting out of there, and Tara needed to be with her, to make sure she got anything she could possibly need.

To make sure she didn't die.

She scooped in a deep breath. "I need to stay with Amour. She's my responsibility."

"You are aware that this wasn't an accident, right?" Xander asked, his dark brown brows lifted so high that they nearly disappeared into his just-long-enough-to-look-hot-instead-of-scruffy hairline.

But not even his hotness, which had grown exponentially since she'd last seen him (along with his shoulders, holy shit) was going to distract her right now.

"Since I was on the phone with her right after it happened, yes. I'm *very* aware of that."

Funny, he seemed totally unmoved by her Lawyer Voice. "Then you're also aware that if you were on the phone with her right after this happened, you *really* need to give a statement as soon as possible so we can try to find the bastard who hurt her."

And *shit*. "She doesn't have any family nearby, and she won't trust anyone else. I need to be with her in case she needs something," Tara said, even though Xander wasn't entirely wrong.

As if he'd sensed her blip of hesitation, he doubled

down, his arms crossing over the front of his body armor. "You need to stay."

"Why don't we do this," said the other officer, a petite Black woman who clearly outranked Xander, if the way he'd just lowered his chin was any indicator. Not that it erased his high-level frown. "I'm going to take a gamble and guess Amour is working something active with you right now. Is that correct?"

The officer, whose nameplate read *L. Dade*, kept her voice barely above a murmur, and Tara nodded.

"That means we do need to act quickly, since we all want the same thing, which is to catch the person who hurt her. At the same time"—Dade lifted a hand to silence the argument that Tara had been concocting, and whoa, that was a powerful, Mom-level, don't-even-think-about-interrupting-me stare—"you are her point of contact, Ms. Kingston, and she's probably going to want a familiar face at the hospital once she's cared for."

Tara swallowed. "She's going to be terrified." Neither Dade nor Xander argued, making Tara's stomach clench. "She's barely eighteen. I really need to go."

This time, Dade sent The Stare at Xander, who looked primed to argue, before saying, "And we really do need a statement...which Officer Matthews is going to get from you before he escorts you to Remington Memorial."

Xander's mouth fell open for a split second before he recovered. "You want *me* to take her statement and escort her to Remington Mem?"

"I do." Dade moved over to the ambulance, thumping the back door twice with her palm to signal an all clear and send the paramedics on their way. "It's going to take the doctors a while to work on Amour, and I know Tess Riley personally. She's the best emergency physician going, but she's not going to let anyone see Amour until they're done, so you have a little time to spare. And since you"— she slid a glance at Xander, who was looking more and more displeased by the minute—"seem to know Ms. Kingston already, you can take her statement and bring her to the hospital. I'll call Sergeant Sinclair to get the Intelligence Unit involved and wait here for the crime scene unit I'm sure he'll roll out. Matthews, you and Ms. Kingston should keep your eyes open for whichever detectives he sends to Mem to get them in the loop. Did I miss anything?"

Tara blinked. "No," she said slowly. "Sinclair knows Amour. She gave us the intel that led to a huge arrest, and she's supposed to testify in six weeks against a guy who wouldn't hesitate to try to hurt her to shut her up."

A frown formed at the corners of Dade's mouth. "I'll be sure to let him know you're making a statement and that you'll be headed to the hospital."

"Thank you," Tara said, then turned toward Xander. "Can we get this over with so I can go?"

She heard her impatience only after it had left her mouth, biting her lip even though it was too late to trap the words so she could rearrange them into something more polite. "I mean, I just—"

"I get it." Lifting one shoulder partway before letting it drop, he gestured to the police cruiser parked in front of the house. "We can do this in the car, if you want. It's probably more comfortable there. Cooler, and all."

In that moment, Tara realized that her blouse was plastered to her body in no less than three places, two of which were her underarms and the third being the too-curvy bust she did her best to hide under normal circumstances.

Xander, of course, looked totally unfazed by the heat

even though he had Kevlar molded to half his beautiful body.

"Fine," she said, making her chin stay level even though she wanted nothing more than to blush her way into the ground. Xander led the way to the cruiser, popping the passenger side door before moving around the vehicle to the driver's side, and Tara sent up a tiny prayer of thanks that the trip kept him from hearing her near-orgasmic moan as the cool interior air hit her skin.

Situating his lean frame in the driver's seat, he pulled out a notepad and pen. "Okay. Why don't we start with where you were when Amour called you tonight?"

"Work," Tara said, as automatically as breathing. "Well, I guess technically, I was leaving work. I was on my way to my car, outside the DA's office, downtown."

Xander was all concentration as he wrote. "And what time was this?"

"Nine thirty. Maybe a few minutes after."

Something that looked a lot like surprise flickered through his light green stare, but he didn't give it voice. "What did she say?"

"I knew right away that something was wrong," Tara said, a chill skating over her forearms at the memory of how Amour's voice had trembled. "She sounded frightened. She asked me to help her."

Tara's voice caught on the last two words, and damn it, she couldn't lose control over this. Not now, and definitely not in front of Xander, who suddenly had the patience of a saint to go with those sinful shoulders.

She cleared her throat and mentally kicked her own ass. "I put her on hold and dialed nine-one-one, then patched her through. I was worried she couldn't do it on her own, and I didn't want to lose her."

Xander nodded. He didn't prompt her or push, and even though Tara knew it was Interview 101 to use as little guidance as possible with a witness, his calm, comforting gaze took a tiny sliver of the tension out of her chest.

"She said she was hurt. The operator asked where she was, and she said she was here. Home." Tara looked at the dilapidated house, with the blue lights throwing eerie shadows over the broken porch boards and the splintered doorframe she could just make out from her spot in the cruiser, her gut dipping. "She said there was a man, but she couldn't tell if he was still there. That her head felt funny. She didn't say much after that. Oh!" The memory slammed into Tara with a burst of awareness. "She said something about what the man had said to her, but she didn't say what it was. She just said, 'he told me not to'."

At that, Xander's brows lifted. "But she didn't say what he told her not to do?"

"No, she must have passed out." Tara stuffed back the fear that went with the thought. She had to be strong. She *had* to. "But Amour is supposed to testify against Ricky Sansone next month, and if he found out she's the informant who gave us the intel that led to his arrest and that she's testifying against him, he wouldn't hesitate to kill her."

"What makes you think that?" Xander asked, and *what?* He had to be kidding.

"Um, don't you think the whole murder/gun-running thing is a bit of a giveaway?"

Xander paused. "I think it's something to explore, yeah. But Amour knows Sansone, right?"

"Of course," Tara said slowly. "She works for him at his club."

"So, if he'd kicked in her door and tried to kill her, she'd probably recognize him," Xander led, and Tara connected the dots with a curse.

"And if she'd recognized him, she *definitely* would've said so on the phone." Still... "Sansone is smart, though. He's out on a million-dollar bond. As badly as he'd want to do the job himself, if he knew Amour was an informant, he wouldn't risk getting caught."

"He also probably wouldn't have left her alive," Xander said, his expression softening at Tara's wince. "Sorry. Did she say anything else that you can think of?"

"No."

Xander shook his head. "Any detail you can remember, even a small one, that might help ID who did this to her?"

Tara's frustration bubbled, and she took a deep breath to counter it. "No."

"A background noise, a voice, maybe? Anything like that?"

Just like that, the last strand of Tara's patience snapped. "*No*. Look, pull the nine-one-one recording if you don't trust me. Then you'll have the whole thing, word for word, complete with background noises and voices and Amour begging for help you can't give her."

Tears pricked her eyes, hot and begging to fall, and oh, no. Not tonight. She would not lose control of this situation, and she sure as *hell* wouldn't be weak enough to cry in front of Xander goddamn Matthews.

A beat passed, then another, before Tara couldn't stand the ear-punching silence or his wide, unreadable stare any longer. "I've told you everything I can remember. Can we go to the hospital now? Please."

"Yes, ma'am," he said, his voice as indecipherable as his stare as he closed his notebook and turned away from her.

3

Xander sat in the luxurious leather passenger seat of Tara's BMW and stared straight at the windshield. They'd traded less than a dozen syllables since he'd finished taking her statement, and those had only included necessary back-and-forth about taking her car to Remington Memorial so she'd have a way home. She hadn't apologized for lighting into him—not that Xander had expected her to. Yeah, he'd only been trying to do his job when he'd questioned her, and yeah again, sometimes the small details that seemed inconsequential could blow a case wide open. But in his eagerness to catch the asshole who'd assaulted Amour, he'd lost sight of the fact that Tara had been on the phone with her directly after it had happened. Listening to someone she clearly cared about in pain. Frightened. Maybe even dying.

Tara might've been unrelentingly tough every other time Xander had clapped eyes on her—including when she'd tried to have him brought up on a laundry list of criminal charges two years ago—but in that moment, she'd been vulnerable. Enough to bring tears to her big, brown eyes.

Tears *he* had put there, albeit inadvertently, and damn it, he needed an olive branch.

"So, ah. Your car is really nice," Xander said, and Christ, as far as olive branches went, that was barely a twig. Also, a colossal understatement, since his ass was currently parked in a seat that had programmable lumbar support *and* a built-in cooling system, in a vehicle that had probably cost more than he'd made in the last two years combined. Maybe three.

Tara blinked and sent him a lightning-fast glance of surprise before saying, "Thank you."

Her delivery was a little on the prim side, but since she hadn't said "fuck you" instead of "thank you", Xander took the tiny victory. "How long have you had it?"

One corner of her mouth lifted into a hint of a sardonic smile. "You don't have to make small talk with me, Xander. I appreciate the courtesy, but I know you probably don't like me very much."

"That's a little extreme," he said, unable to tell if he was more shocked or turned on by her lack of tolerance for anything resembling bullshit.

Tara shrugged. "Considering tonight's circumstances, I wouldn't blame you if it were still accurate."

"Still," Xander repeated. He hooked the end of the word upward until it became a question, and Tara's dark auburn brows popped.

"Well, yes. I assumed there was already no love lost from two years ago."

Fuck. He should've known the past wouldn't *stay* in the past. It never goddamn did. "That was a long time ago."

Tara fell for the way he'd notched his tone right at its most easygoing setting, because she said, "Maybe. But my office still tried to send you to jail for a really long time."

"Bygones." Xander realized he'd sent the word through his teeth, and damn it, he needed to breathe. "It all turned out fine in the end."

The look on her face said she wanted to argue (hello, attorney), but Xander about-faced the subject. "Anyway, I owe you an apology for tonight."

"What?" Tara breathed. Under any other circumstances, he might've gotten a thrill at shocking her thoroughly enough to make her ridiculously lush mouth fall open like that. But he stood the ground he'd just stolen.

"Amour is your CI, and you two obviously have a good relationship. Interview protocol is designed to gain useful information, not overwhelm the person being questioned. I overstepped when I kept pushing you for details, and for that, I'm sorry."

"Oh." Tara paused, and in less than a blink, the uncharacteristic softness in her expression got back to business. "Well, don't be. I'm not."

Xander's laugh held equal parts humor and disbelief. "Okay, not to put too fine a point on it, because I do have *some* pride, but you handed me my lunch back there. Respectfully, I'm not really sure I'm buying that you're not sorry I pushed."

She pulled to a stop at the red light in front of them before lifting one hand from the wheel in a wordless translation of *mea culpa*. "I was a bit...brash. But it's not as if I don't know the process for giving a statement, and that it needs to be thorough. You were just doing your job, and I was"—she trailed off for a beat, then one more before turning to look at him through the shadowy interior of the car—"Well, I should've reacted differently."

A burst of desire moved through Xander, swift and enticingly hot, and Christ, was he nuts? This woman drove a BMfucking-W and was a smart, successful attorney in the DA's office. She wasn't for him. Not fleetingly. Not just in his head.

Not ever.

Xander smoothed his expression and tugged together all the no-big-deal he could muster. Once he delivered Tara to the hospital and relayed her statement and an update to the Intelligence Unit detectives who would surely meet them there, the chances were high he wouldn't even see her again. All he had to do was make it through the next hour or so. Then he could go back to keeping his head down and his ass in his own lane.

"What do you say we just call it even?" he asked, extending his hand over the center console.

Tara looked at him, her copper-colored eyes as wide as pennies but her grasp firm as she wrapped her fingers around his and shook.

"I'd say you've got yourself a clean slate."

Oh, if only. Nothing about him was ever going to be clean.

Especially with a woman like Tara Kingston.

The rest of the ride passed in comfortable silence, with Xander trying to get the image of her sexy, sassy mouth out of his head and Tara blissfully unaware of his wicked (and wickedly inappropriate) thoughts. Remington Memorial's Emergency Department was relatively quiet, with only a handful of people spread out across the waiting room, and Tara didn't waste any time heading for the intake desk.

"I'm Tara Kingston, with the DA's office. I'm here for a patient who was brought in via ambulance. Amour Pollard. Aimee," she added, and the scrubs-clad man behind the desk nodded.

"The paramedics said to expect you. Dr. Riley is with the

patient right now. You'll have to wait out here." He darted an apologetic glance at the waiting room. "But I'll let her know you're here. She'll come find you as soon as she can."

Tara tensed beside him in a way that said she was primed to argue, and Xander edged his way into her line of vision before he could stop himself. "Tara, she's in the best hands. You don't want to mess with that," he said quietly. "Plus, we have to wait for someone from Intelligence to get here to work this case before we can do anything, anyway. It's SOP, and we have to do this by the book."

To his total surprise, she eked out a small, slow nod. Thanking the intake nurse, she stepped back with a frown. "I know you're right. But..."

"The waiting sucks. I know." Xander slapped back the memory of exactly how well-acquainted he was with that particular terror and gestured toward the chairs. "Do you want to sit down? It might be a while."

"Not really, no."

"Okay." Xander tried Door Number Two. "Maybe we should find a vending machine. Are you hungry?"

Tara shook her head, knocking a strand of hair loose from the already tousled twist pinned just behind her ear. "No, thank you. I just want to wait right here for Dr. Riley."

She locked her fingers together and started to pace. Her shoes—a pair of classy black heels with slim straps around her ankles that did absolutely zip for Xander's composure—clipped a steady rhythm over the linoleum, and after the third circuit of pacing/hand wringing, he realized he was going to have to stage an intervention, otherwise she was going to fry her own circuitry before Dr. Riley could get even close to an update.

He fell into step alongside her. "Interesting story. Like,

thirty years ago, there was this cargo ship on its way from Hong Kong to the United States."

"What?" Tara stopped short to stare at him, but Xander didn't let go of his steady-as-she-goes expression.

"Cargo ship. Hong Kong to the U.S.," he repeated. When she was too shocked to verbalize the WTF that was scribbled all over her pretty face, he continued. "On the route, the ship accidentally lost a shipping crate, like, smack in the middle of the Pacific Ocean. I bet you can't guess what was in it."

She blinked. "Electronics?"

"Good guess, but no."

"Car parts." A competitive spark lit her eyes, making her even prettier than usual.

Xander forced his shoulders into a haphazard shrug and his dick to stand down. "Nope."

"Clothing?"

"Not even close."

"Xander." His name was all warning as it crossed Tara's lips, and he had to cave.

"Twenty-eight thousand rubber ducks."

The look on her face was priceless. "I'm sorry. Did you say—"

"Yup. Ducks. So, the shipping company figures they're lost, right? I mean, the crate fell into the ocean." He pantomimed a big splash with his hands. "But then these rubber ducks started popping up in all sorts of places."

"Are you serious?" Tara asked, fully hooked on the story if her expression was anything to go by.

Annnd gotcha. "Scout's honor," he said, even though he was as far from a Boy Scout as a man could get. "Australia. Alaska. The shores of the Atlantic. They've even found a couple frozen in Arctic ice."

"No way." She huffed out a laugh. "That's thousands of miles."

"I know, right? But that's the coolest part. Those accidental ducks ended up teaching marine researchers a ton about ocean currents. A few still pop up here and there to this day."

"Oh, my God, that's so cool," Tara murmured. The ease on her face lasted for a beat, then one more before her chin whipped up, and ah, busted. "You did that on purpose, didn't you?"

Xander slid on his poker face like it was his Sunday best. "I'm not sure what you mean."

"You used that story to distract me so I'd relax."

Her hands found the generous curve of her hips, and Xander wondered if the move was pure reflex. *Focus. And not on grabbing her hips while fucking her senseless.* "Uh," Xander grunted, and what the hell was *wrong* with him? "Yeah, maybe. But you weren't going to last five minutes pacing the floor like that, and I know you want to save your energy for Amour."

Tara took a step toward him, her arms softening at her sides. "You're a really nice guy, you know that?"

The urge to correct her was strong, but Xander bit it in half and said, "Just doing my job."

"The standard answer when someone says 'you're a nice guy' is usually 'thank you'."

The words carried none of her usual heat, filled instead with curiosity, and hell, Xander would take her ire a million times over the beautiful, wide-open look on her face right now. "Thank you."

Another step, and now Tara was right in front of him, close enough to touch. "How come you don't like being called a nice guy?"

His pulse flared, but that shit about old habits was real.

This time, he stepped toward *her*, cutting the distance between them to inches. "The standard answer when someone says 'thank you' is usually 'you're welcome'."

"Oh," Tara breathed. Her lips parted to release the sound as a sigh, and suddenly, there was nothing in the universe other than him, her, and the red-hot urge to claim her mouth. "You're welcome, Xander."

"Hey, you two. Hope we're not interrupting?"

The female voice—not Tara's, but almost as close by—whiplashed Xander back down to earth. "No," he and Tara said simultaneously, both of them taking gargantuan steps away from each other.

By the time Xander turned toward Intelligence Detectives Isabella Walker and Matteo Garza, his nothing-to-see-here armor was firmly back in place. "Not at all. Ms. Kingston and I were just killing time, waiting for you guys to arrive."

"Right." Isabella's smile told Xander she saw right through him (freaking detectives), so he went for old faithful.

"Hey, you look great, by the way." He gestured to her rounded belly. "How far along are you now?"

Whether or not she was onto him, she took the bait. "Six months, and I look like I gulped down a basketball. But you're a doll for lying." Isabella took a second to run her hand lovingly over her baby bump before getting to the matter at hand. "And I'm still allowed to do victim interviews even if I have to take a break from *actively* chasing criminals, which is what Hollister is doing right now, the lucky brat"—she gave up a tart smile at the mention of her partner, Liam Hollister—"so I'm tagging along with Garza, here, in order to feel useful. Do you want to give us the rundown?"

Xander nodded and got down to business. "Aimee Pollard, goes by Amour, eighteen, assaulted in her home in North Point." He rolled through the bullet, making sure to take pit stops at the head injury, no outward signs of sexual assault, and Amour's phone call to Tara. "Dr. Riley's with her now. No update yet."

"Shit," Garza said, dividing his dark gaze between Isabella and Tara. "You think Sansone's behind this?"

"Who else would it be?" Tara asked. "You both worked that case. You know what she risked to get us that intel. *And* what he's capable of. If he knows she's the one who gave us what we needed to get him arrested, he wouldn't hesitate to hurt her."

Slowly, Isabella said, "We do have to look at every angle. Amour doesn't exactly live in the safest of neighborhoods, and break-ins that end in assault aren't unusual in North Point. This could just be a robbery gone wrong or a home invasion. That said"—she looked at Tara, who had already opened her mouth to argue—"I agree that the whole thing is pretty freaking suspicious. Something about this doesn't quite pass the smell test. But we won't know what until we can talk to Amour."

"I'm not about to go back there and piss Tess off," Garza said, and Xander silently agreed. The doctor was part of a larger group of first responders and medical staff who hung out at his sister Kennedy's bar on the regular, and while Tess had always seemed nice enough outside of the hospital, the stories of how she ran her ED without an ounce of bullshit and even less apology were practically lore. Plus, she was married to a guy who used to jump out of helicopters. On purpose. *Repeatedly.*

"She knows we're here," Xander said quietly. "And she knows Amour is the victim of a crime. She'll come find us as soon as she can."

At that, a tart laugh sounded off from over Garza's brawny shoulder, and they all turned to see Tess Riley standing there in her dark green scrubs and doctor's coat.

"Give the rookie a gold star. And I'm glad the gang's all here, because we need to talk."

4

All the emotion Tara had managed to tamp down came rushing up in full force, taking the last shred of her decorum with it.

"Tell me she's okay," she said past her heart, which was lodged firmly in her throat and pounding like a jackhammer.

The woman—Dr. Riley, according to the name stitched on her white doctor's coat—took a lightning-fast look at Tara before saying, "I'm going to assume you're Tara?"

At Tara's nod, Dr. Riley continued. "Amour said you'd probably be assertive."

All the air left Tara's lungs on a rush of relief. *She's not dead. Not like Lucas.* "She said that?"

"Actually, her exact words were, 'She's probably going to lose her shit if you don't go get her', but I figured assertive works, too," the doctor said over a smile. "For the record, assertive is my favorite quality, and yes, Amour is okay. She's a pretty tough cookie."

"What can you tell us about her injury?" Detective Garza asked, his dark eyes as serious as his expression.

Dr. Riley wasted no time ushering them past a set of double doors and farther into the ED for privacy. "She's awake and stable, although she's pretty woozy and obviously shaken. She didn't say much about what happened, and I didn't want to agitate her by pushing until I ruled out a skull fracture or more serious brain injury. All signs point to no on both of those right now, but I called in a neuro consult, just to be safe." She directed the gentler words at Tara before putting some frost into her tone. "Whoever assaulted her knew what they were doing. Amour sustained blunt force trauma to the right temple resulting in a moderate concussion, along with some lesser-degree facial trauma to the nose and contusions to her neck and upper extremities."

Tara's gut bottomed out in dread. "He *choked* her before he hit her?"

"Son of a bitch," Isabella bit out. "So, whoever did this was a lot stronger than she is?"

"And taller, too," Dr. Riley agreed. "From the angle of the shot to the temple, I'd say your assailant is at least six inches taller than Amour, and that's a minimum."

"So, probably male," Garza said.

"And left-handed," Xander pointed out, and Isabella nodded.

"That's likely, given that Amour's worst injury is to her right temple. Any idea if he used a weapon for the shot to the head?"

Dr. Riley's frown grew. "He definitely used something other than his fists. I can't be a hundred percent sure what, but in my expert medical opinion...it looks like a pretty classic pistol-whip."

Oh, God.

Tara must've spoken the gut-clenching words out loud, because Xander shot her one of those calm, cool, *everything's going to be okay* gazes, just as he had before he'd thrown her for a loop with that rubber duck story. "But you said she's okay now?"

"The neurology resident was with her when I left, but she's stable. At this point, I'd feel more comfortable keeping her until morning, just to be on the safe side and make sure she keeps to the concussion protocol. It wouldn't hurt for someone from psych to try to talk to her, too. Trauma victims don't just have to heal from their physical injuries."

"I want to stay with her," Tara said. Amour was tough, but God, Dr. Riley was right. The poor girl had just been assaulted in her own house. Tara might hate hospitals with the red-hot intensity of a thousand fiery suns, but... "I don't want her to be alone. Plus, once Sansone finds out he didn't kill her, who knows what he might try to do."

Garza swapped looks with Isabella, but Tara didn't know either detective well enough to read between the unspoken lines. "Let's take this one step at a time. We have to prove it was Sansone first. Tess, do you think Amour is up for an interview? The sooner we do this, the sooner we can start figuring out who hurt her."

"It'll have to be quick, and if she gets too overwhelmed, we'll have to cut it off. I know she's tough, but I also know I don't need to remind you she's had a hell of a night."

"Understood," Isabella said. Turning toward Xander, she asked, "You sticking around to sharpen your victim interview skills, Matthews?"

"Yes, ma'am." His nod sent the weirdest shot of relief through Tara's chest. "I'd like to see this one through, as long as that's alright with you."

Garza jerked his chin. "Never hurts to learn, but do us a favor, both of you, and let us do our job? This case in under Intelligence's jurisdiction until we can make an arrest."

Tara bristled, but before she could tell Tall, Dark, and Broody exactly where he could shove his jurisdiction, Isabella said, "I think what Garza, here, is trying to say in his own charming way is, we really have to be sure we do this by the book. Especially if Sansone is involved. The last thing we want to do is give his lawyer any sort of technicality to hang a dismissal on."

And Sansone's attorney was the slimiest defense lawyer dirty money could buy. *Shit.* "Understood," Tara muttered.

"Okay," Dr. Riley said, leading them toward an exam room at the far end of the hallway. "I'll stick to the background in case she needs anything. Try to be quick?"

"Of course," Isabella promised. Turning toward Tara, she said, "You're good for this, right?"

Tara nodded even though her heart was screaming to the contrary. "I have to be. Amour needs an advocate. I won't let her down."

With that, she headed past the exam room door and slid the privacy curtain aside. Her pulse took an immediate roller coaster ride at the sight of Amour on the gurney in the center of the room, the dim lights casting dark shadows beneath her eyes, deepening the bruises already forming there. Her blond hair was matted and pulled back, yielding to the mass of gauze covering the right side of her face, and Tara choked down the noise her throat wanted to make.

"Hey, Amour," she murmured, marshaling her voice to steadiness she sure as shit didn't feel. "Are you up for visitors?"

The young woman blinked her eyes open, looking startled. "Tara?"

"It's me," Tara assured her, moving swiftly to the gurney to scoop up Amour's hand. Damn it, she was trembling. "I'm right here with Detectives Walker and Garza, from Intelligence. Do you remember them?"

Amour bit her lip. "Yeah." Her eyes darted to Xander, who had hung back behind Isabella. "I remember you, too. You were there. Holding my head, after."

Xander took one step forward, but still stayed far from Amour's personal space. "Yes, ma'am. Officer Matthews. Would it be okay with you if I stay while you talk to the detectives? I'd really like to make sure you're alright."

"Oh." Amour blinked, then lifted a too-thin shoulder partway before letting it drop. "Sure, I guess. I'm fine, but whatever."

"You gave us a bit of a scare, kid," Garza said as he moved to Amour's other side, his gruff demeanor replaced by a look of empathy so deep, it shocked Tara. "How are you feeling?"

"I just want to get this over with," she said, her hand starting to shake again despite the steel she'd tried to put in her voice.

A frown flickered over Garza's face, and yeah, that made two of them. "Okay. Can you tell us what happened?"

"I don't remember anything," Amour said, her words nearly crashing into Garza's, and okay, something about this didn't wash.

"You just said you remember Officer Matthews," Tara pointed out, ignoring the way Garza's jaw tightened beneath his five o'clock shadow. For Chrissake, she'd graduated in the top ten in her class at Stanford. She wasn't going to ask anything that would give Sansone's lawyer, as scummy as the guy was, an advantage.

Amour paused. "I don't remember anything about the guy who did this."

"Except that it was a guy," Isabella said. Gently, she added, "Amour, we want to help you."

"Well, you can't," she said, her eyes filling with angry tears, and in that instant, it clicked.

"He threatened you."

At Amour's wide-eyed stare in reply, Tara continued, "Amour, listen to me. If Sansone did this to you, we can go to the judge and get an order of protection. With your testimony, we can—"

"It wasn't him."

Tara tried again. "Amour, I know you're—"

"Tara, you're not listening. It wasn't *him*."

"But someone threatened you," Garza said, and Amour finally eked out a tiny nod.

"This guy was big. Bigger than Sansone. Like you." Her stare flickered over Garza before dropping to the thin blanket draped over her lap. The detective had to be six foot two, and he'd definitely eaten his Wheaties as a kid, because damn, he wasn't coming up short in the muscles department. "I was in the kitchen, getting a drink. I've been working a lot of late nights, so I wanted to crash early, but then I heard footsteps on the porch. I barely had time to turn around before the door came crashing in."

Amour paused for a shaky breath. "I ran to my bedroom. I know it was dumb, but he was blocking the front door, so it's not like I could get out that way, and my phone was on my nightstand, charging. He caught me before I could get to it, though."

This time, her pause lapsed into silence, which Garza filled with, "You're doing great, Amour. This is giving us a really good idea of what happened."

Whether the encouragement worked or she just wanted to be done with her statement, Tara couldn't tell. But Amour kept going. "He grabbed me by the tops of my arms and hit me once in the face, really hard. I was so surprised, I couldn't do anything. I couldn't even scream. It was like I was just stuck there. So stupid."

"That's a very common reaction," Isabella offered gently. "And it's very likely that he hit you for just that reason— because he knew you'd probably freeze. Did you manage to get a good look at him?"

"No." She shrugged. "He was wearing a ski mask and a hoodie. Maybe jeans? I don't remember."

"That's okay," Garza said. "What about his hands? Could you tell what color his skin was?"

Recognition lit Amour's eyes, and Tara squeezed her fingers in encouragement. "He was wearing gloves, but when he grabbed me, the cuffs of his hoodie slid up a little. He was white, and I could see a tattoo. Not a lot, but it had numbers. What do you call them, when you keep count with those lines?"

"Hash marks?" Tara supplied, and Amour nodded, just once before realizing her concussion made it the worst sort of idea.

"Yeah. I tried to get away from him, but he put his hands around my throat and squeezed, just enough to make it hard to breathe unless I was really still. And he said..."

Amour broke off, the tears that had been hanging on to her lashes finally spilling over her face. "I can't. I can't tell you." She looked at Tara. "I'm sorry."

Tara's heart vaulted against her breastbone, and she fought for composure. "Amour, listen to me. We can keep you safe. Whatever he said—"

"You *can't*," she insisted, pulling her hand out of Tara's, her defenses locked and loaded in her glare. "You don't understand. He knows where I live. Where I work. What I did! He's fucking crazy, Tara. Nobody can keep me safe from that but *me*. I'm not telling you what he said, and I'm not testifying in court. I'm done with all of it."

Oh, no. No, no. "Amour—"

"Save your breath, girl."

"Amour," Isabella tried.

"*No!*"

The half-shout was enough to snare Dr. Riley's attention. "Okay, that's enough. Either we get a whole lot more chill about this or interview time is over."

Tara battled the panic starting to rise in her chest. Amour wouldn't be safe unless they got this guy and Sansone—who had surely hired or bribed this guy to scare her—behind bars, permanently, and without Amour's cooperation, they were screwed. She had to do something, God, *anything*, to get her to talk. "Amour—"

"It's pretty scary, isn't it?"

Xander's voice slipped through the tension in the room, surprising the hell out of Tara.

Amour, too, if the look on her face was anything to go by. "What?"

"I said, it's pretty scary, being threatened like you were tonight." He stepped a little further out of the shadows, but still didn't come close to Amour's personal space, as if he wanted to give her literal room to breathe.

She eyed him with tough disdain. "What do you know about it? You're a fucking cop."

"I'm also a Northie, born and raised. And I know exactly what you're feeling, because two years ago, I was in the same situation."

Amour eyed him with a solid dose of mistrust, but enough curiosity flickered through her stare that no one intervened. "*You're* a Northie?"

"Lived on The Hill for most of my life. Sullivan Street," he added, and Amour's brows lifted.

"In that apartment building by the park?"

"Where all the junkies hang out at night," Xander confirmed. "And the pawn shop on the corner, by Old Lou's market."

Amour remained wary, but she kept talking. "I know it. Old Lou's not bad."

"He used to give me and my sister milk on the expiration day when we were tight on money. He's a good guy. Mean as a snake if you mess with his candy displays, though."

"So, what happened to you?" Amour asked, and Tara had to admit her curiosity was burning through her, too.

Xander said, "I got jammed up with someone I shouldn't have—you know how it is. You've gotta make a living, and you can't look sideways in North Point without your eyes landing on someone with crappy intentions."

Amour huffed out a laugh, although it carried very little joy. "Yeah. I don't exactly love wearing a leather bustier and getting groped for shitty tips, but..."

She shrugged off the rest, and Xander filled in the blanks all too smoothly. "You don't exactly have great options. So, you keep your head down and try to make things work. But then a guy like Ricky Sansone comes along, doing all sorts of nasty stuff to people, and the next thing you know, you're in over your head."

Isabella and Garza seemed all too happy to let Xander go with the lead he'd so smoothly taken, and Tara watched, half-mesmerized, as Amour nodded.

"He was hurting people, putting guns on the street. North Point is bad enough, you know? Most of us have enough shit to worry about without having to dodge bullets, so when I saw the chance to put him away..."

She broke off. Xander's expression never wavered, as if he had nothing in the world more important to do than sit there and wait until she was ready to keep going.

And she did. "But I was supposed to be safe. I didn't sign on for *this*." She waved a hand around the exam room. Xander took a careful step forward until he was right beside the gurney, never dropping eye contact with her.

"Believe me, I get it. I have the scars to prove it, too." Rolling up his right uniform sleeve, he revealed a two-inch burn scar that made Tara's heart race. "I was scared out of my head the whole time."

"But you got out," Amour said, with just enough curiosity for Xander to take the opening she'd given him.

"I did, but in order to make it work, I had to do something that scared me almost more than the person who did this to me. I had to be honest with *these* guys." He hooked a thumb over his shoulder in Isabella and Garza's direction. "Look, none of us can tell you what to do. What you say or don't say in this interview is entirely up to you. But I can tell you this. Telling these detectives the truth saved my life, and I know that if you're honest with them, they'll do everything in their power to save yours."

The silence that stretched through the exam room felt like it lasted for a month before Amour broke it with, "Would...would you help them keep me safe for real? *If* I wanted to talk, I mean."

Tara's chest tightened with hope, and it took every single shred of her self-control not to interject.

"These detectives are the real pros, Amour," Xander said,

looking at Garza and Isabella with a nod. "But if I can help them in any way, I will."

"I'm here, too." Tara squeezed Amour's hand. "I promise."

Letting out a slow breath, Amour said, "Okay. I'll tell you everything."

Xander walked into the lounge Tess had cleared for their group and bit back a curse. True to her word, Amour had told them exactly what her assailant had said as he'd wrapped his fingers around her throat.

You've been running that filthy mouth of yours, haven't you, you little whore? Xander was helpless against the soundtrack in his head, the one that had played on an endless loop ever since Amour had set it into motion.

"I told him I didn't know what he was talking about," she'd said. "But he just squeezed tighter."

You know exactly what I'm talking about. Either you shut your cock-sucking mouth or I will find you. I will rip out your tongue so you can't scream, and I will cut off every one of your fingers so you can't fight back. I will violate you in every way possible, and it will *hurt. But not as bad as when I cut up the rest of you once I'm done. Do you understand?*

She'd said yes.

He'd pistol-whipped her on his way out the door anyway.

"Okay," Isabella said, breaking Xander's gut-clenching rewind. "I've gotten Sergeant Sinclair up to speed, but obviously, this is going to be a high-priority case."

Sinclair, who had arrived just as they'd been finishing up their interview with Amour, ran a hand over his gray-blond crew cut. "That may be understating it. Threatening an informant isn't exactly unexpected for someone in Sansone's situation, but it *is* serious. I've spoken with your boss"—he looked at Tara—"and he made it clear that he believes the threat is real."

Xander silently agreed. Amour's injuries were proof positive. What the guy who had delivered them had said as he'd done it? Even worse.

Tara raised a coppery brow, her expression pure *are you kidding me?* "Of course the threat is real. But"—she paused to bite her bottom lip in a move that Xander would have to be pulse-free not to notice—"Sansone clearly knows Amour is our CI, and he *very* clearly wants her out of the picture so she won't testify. Why not just have her killed? It's not as if this guy didn't have the chance."

"It isn't one he can take," Isabella said. "If Amour ends up dead, he knows we'll come crawling up his ass with a microscope, and he doesn't want that kind of heat. But if she decides not to testify..."

This time, Xander let his curse fly under his breath. "Then the case falls apart and he walks."

"I wouldn't put it past him to tie up loose ends after that happens, either. Sansone was a nasty SOB the first time we went after him," Garza said, and Sinclair nodded his agreement.

"Well, now he's nasty *and* smart. Whoever he got to do his dirty work tonight knew exactly what to say to make this case an uphill climb."

"More like what not to say," Tara muttered. "The man who assaulted Amour never said Sansone's name. Never mentioned the case, or anything even related to it. Sansone's attorney will argue that he has no idea what we're talking about. And I'd bet a Maserati that he's got an airtight alibi for tonight, with no less than ten witnesses who can put him across the city from Amour's house."

"We've broken cases open with less," Isabella said. "One good thing about riding a desk is that I have plenty of time to go over every inch of this case. Video surveillance, forensics from Amour's house, witness statements. Name it, and I'm in."

"That's a good start," Sinclair said, and Xander had to agree. Isabella had some of the sharpest eyes he'd ever seen. "We'll have to do the obligatory meet-and-greet with Sansone and his attorney. Who's presiding over the case?"

Tara made a face. "Alana Waters. Look up Stickler in the dictionary, and her face will be right there, front and center."

"That bad?" Xander asked.

Tara snorted in time with the Intelligence detectives' nods. "She once corrected my grammar while I was arguing against a dismissal in her chambers."

Ouch. Still... "Okay, but no one can deny that Amour's life was threatened."

"It doesn't matter if we can't prove Sansone's the one behind it," Tara said. "The first step *is* getting on the record with Judge Waters, though. I'm going to have to figure out how to get Amour to agree to testify, but keeping her safe is a good place to start."

Garza lifted his chin in agreement. "Capelli's already working on getting her into protective custody." At the mention of the Intelligence Unit's tech and surveillance guru, Tara's shoulders seemed to relax by a fraction. "But he's running into an issue finding a good place with immediate availability."

The RPD kept a handful of places on tap for protective custody, offsite surveillance and ops planning, and other various and sundry tasks that required the utmost secrecy, Xander knew. Apparently, they were all in use.

"What about an extended-stay motel?" Tara asked, but Sergeant Sinclair shook his head.

"That's six weeks' worth of variables we can't predict. Staff who could be pressured or bribed. It's too risky for a case this big."

"There's a vacant apartment on my floor," Xander said, only realizing he was going to put the thought to words after it had bolted past his lips. But now everyone in the room was staring at him, so great. Guess he was running with it. "The guy who lived down the hall from me moved out a couple days ago. The building is pretty nice. No doorman to worry about, but all residents need a keycard to get in and guests have to be buzzed through, so the security's pretty tight."

Isabella's brows lifted as she slid a look at Sinclair. "That's not a half-bad idea. I know the building—Gamble used to live there, right?"

Xander nodded. He'd taken over the lease at his brother-in-law's place when the guy had moved in with Xander's sister a couple years ago.

"It's over on Delancey, about fifteen minutes from the fire house," Isabella said for everyone else's benefit. "As good a location as any for something like this. And it would keep Amour close."

"Let's schedule a walk-through first thing in the morning," Sinclair said. "Amour's going to have to stay here overnight anyway. Dr. Riley runs a clean ship, but we'll put an officer outside her room, just in case. But if this apartment pans out, we'll have Capelli roll through it with all the bells and whistles so we can get Amour in there as soon as possible."

Tara put her hands on her hips, accentuating both her determination and her curves. "I'm staying with her until she's released. She's already rattled, and telling her she has to go into protective custody is only going to prove how much danger she's in. She needs an anchor."

"Lucky for her, she's getting two," Sinclair said, prompting a whole lot of WTF to cross Tara's features.

And that made two of them. "What?" Xander asked.

Sinclair turned to pin him into place with a steely gray stare. "Isabella told me you earned Amour's trust during her interview."

Shock twisted through Xander's rib cage, and he made every attempt to keep it far from his expression. "Yes, sir, but—"

"Nothing," Sinclair finished smoothly. "It worked. She asked for help from you, specifically. I'm not inclined to tell her no. Unless you feel like you're not up for working this case?"

Telling Sinclair no would be the most permanent sort of career suicide. Dade would probably murder him with her thumbs alone if he passed this up, and that was only if his sister didn't do it first. Plus, the whole reason he'd signed on to be a cop in the first place was to help people who needed it, just like he had two years ago.

So he opened his mouth and said, "Not at all, sir. I'm happy to be on the team."

So much for keeping his head down and his ass far, far away from Tara Kingston.

"ALEXANDER TRENTON MATTHEWS, get your ass to the back of this bar right this instant!"

Xander winced, swinging a gaze through The Crooked Angel's dining room as he made his way to the bar per his sister's demand. "A little louder, Ken. There are a few people in the next county who didn't quite catch my middle name."

His brother-in-law looked up from his usual spot at the end of the bar and shook his head. "I wouldn't fuck with her right now," Gamble murmured quietly, turning to give Xander a handshake and a slap on the shoulder.

"I can hear you, you know," Kennedy said, although Xander noticed her expression went way soft as she let her gaze flicker over her husband.

"I know, baby." One corner of Gamble's mouth kicked up into a smile. "But you love me and my smart mouth, remember?"

Annnnd welcome to the awkward portion of the evening. "*I* can hear you, you know," Xander offered up, and Kennedy leveled him with a glare.

"Don't think you're getting out of this, Xander. Why did I have to hear that you're working a high-profile case with the Intelligence Unit from my girlfriends five *days* after the fact, instead of getting that *ginormous* piece of information straight from the horse's mouth, hmm?"

Damn it. He should've figured both Isabella and Quinn would mention this case to his sister, at least tangentially. "Because I'm not supposed to talk about the details?" Thank God it was still early enough for the bar to be mostly empty.

Kennedy didn't budge by as much as a millimeter. "And I know better than to ask for them. Still, a little 'oh, by the

way, I'm working a case with the most elite unit in the city'
wouldn't have killed you, would it?"

"It is kind of a big deal, dude," Gamble chimed in. "Sinclair doesn't let just anybody run assists with that unit. You
must have done something pretty badass to earn your way
in. Even temporarily."

Yeah, it was time to knock this conversation down a peg
or ten. "Honestly, I was just doing my job. Which is why I'm
here, actually. Can I place an order for carry out?"

Amour might not be able to leave the one-bedroom
apartment six doors down from his, but she could at least
have a decent comfort meal. Xander had mostly been on
surveillance and security detail this week, keeping her safe
from a distance while she was in protective custody. The
apartment—with the exception of the bathroom—was
wired to the nines thanks to Capelli's handiwork, but
Sinclair wasn't one to fuck around. Having Xander keep an
eye on the block from various vantage points at different
times of the day and night ensured that they had a handle
on anyone suspicious lingering around.

So far, Xander's job had been chock-full of a whole lot of
nothing-to-see-here. Which would be great...if the investigation wasn't also yielding the same brand of results.

Never one not to feed him, Kennedy sighed and wrote
down his order. "So, you can't tell me any details. Which I
guess I get," she added grudgingly. "But can you at least tell
me how working with Tara Kingston is going? She's not
giving you a hard time, is she?"

More like a hard-*on*. Not that Xander was going to let
that little nugget of truth fly, least of all to his sister.
"Nope. I haven't really seen her much since we set
this up."

Specifically, he'd seen her three times for a total of seven minutes, and she'd looked gorgeous enough to knock the breath out of him each time.

Not that he was counting.

"So, you two didn't have a *moment*?" Kennedy pressed, and shit, he knew that look.

"I have no idea what that means," Xander said, but his sister had never once let him off the hook for something like this. Of course she wasn't going to choose today to go all new leaf.

"Isabella said that when she and Garza showed up to do an interview, you and Tara were standing toe to toe, looking all 'intense'."

Ah, hell. Isabella had some of the keenest eyes in Remington. Of course she'd picked up on all the hot-and-heavy that had been snapping between him and Tara like an electrical current when she and Garza had arrived. But it had just been an off moment, fueled by an overage of adrenaline and emotion. Over and done.

"You've met Tara," Xander said carefully. "Intense is probably her middle name. But it wasn't a big deal."

Kennedy snapped a bar towel from the half-apron around her waist and swiped it over the bar. "It had better not be."

Before Xander could voice the surprise pinging through his system, Gamble intervened. "Kingston came at you pretty hard a couple years ago. We just want to be sure that's all still in the rearview. Where it belongs."

The reminder stuck between Xander's ribs, but at least he could use this to his advantage.

He shrugged. "Oh, that. Yeah, everything between me and Tara is fine. We're both pretty focused on working this case, so, you know. Can't waste energy getting personal about business."

No matter how badly he still wanted to kiss her. Hard and fast and so fucking deep, he could taste every inch of her smart, sassy mouth.

A flicker of something Xander couldn't readily identify moved through Gamble's stare. "You sure everything's okay between you and Kingston?" he asked.

"Absolutely," Xander said, dismissing all thoughts of Tara's mouth as he tugged on a smile. A woman like that, with her high-class law degree and fancy car, wasn't ever going to be for a guy like him. He needed to stop thinking about her, once and for all. "So, how have things been going here? Business good?"

"Oh, ah. Yep," Kennedy stammered, clearly thrown by the change in subject. "Business is, you know. Totally as usual. Absolutely nothing new."

She exchanged a look with Gamble, both of them pausing just long enough to make Xander's bullshit detector explode.

"You want to try again?" he asked, worry sinking into his chest. "What's going on?"

Kennedy looked at the ceiling, the slim platinum barbell in her eyebrow glinting in the bar lights. "I told you," she whispered to Gamble, and wait...were those *tears* in his sister's eyes? Hadn't she just been cranky with him? And worried? And—news flash—she never, *ever* cried.

Unless something was terribly, horribly wrong.

"Okay, you're starting to freak me out," Xander said, standing up so he could meet her gaze head-on. "Seriously. What's wrong?"

Gamble smiled, the sort of huge, ear-to-ear affair that Xander had seen on the guy maybe twice before in his life, and holy shit, this whole thing had officially gone Twilight Zone. "Babe, it's okay. Just tell him."

"We're not supposed to! Ugh, this whole thing is so stupid. They need to *warn* people it's going to be like this," Kennedy said, gesturing to the tears rolling down her face.

Xander took a deep breath and did his best not to use it to scream. "Will one of you please tell me what's going on? Are you sick or something?"

"No. No one is sick," Gamble said, looking at Kennedy, who finally put Xander out of his misery.

"We're having a baby."

Xander stopped. Rewound. Processed her words once, then again, before—

"Oh, shit! Are you serious?" If anyone was cut out to be the world's best mom, it was Kennedy. And Gamble as a dad? Hell, yes. "This is great. Why didn't you want to tell me?"

"There are, like, *millions* of websites that say you're not supposed to tell anyone until after the first trimester," Kennedy said. "But that's a whole three weeks from now! My doctor said the baby looks healthy, and I am obviously a fountain of fucking hormones over here"—she swiped at her face while Gamble nodded vigorously—"and you're my brother and I love you and yes. I suck at keeping secrets from you. So, you're going to be an uncle."

"Can I hug you?" Xander asked, teasing her with his smile. "Or are there, like, *millions* of websites that say you shouldn't hug your brother after you share your happy news with him?"

"You're an asshole," Kennedy said, starting to cry again. "Now, yes. Get over here and hug me, because I need it."

"Man, you weren't kidding about the hormones, huh?" Xander asked from the side of his mouth, and Gamble shook his head.

"You have no idea."

It wasn't until after Kennedy had hugged him and filled him in on all the details that were fit to share about the baby, then handed over his carryout order and hugged him one more time goodbye, that Xander realized the look on Gamble's face when he'd said things were just business between him and Tara had been doubt.

6

T ara dropped her spoon into the empty bowl in front of her and frowned. "Are you sure you don't need anything else?"

Amour looked up from the mostly full bowl of ice cream she'd been trailing her spoon through and shook her head. "Nah. I'm good."

Tara considered calling the younger woman out on the lie. She'd been here for an hour, catching Amour up on the investigation (condensed version: still no solid leads, but Intelligence was working the case from every angle) and making sure she was okay (news flash: she'd been assaulted and had her life threatened by someone who very much meant to kill her. Okay was a pipe dream). Amour might be safe, but she'd been pretty listless for the duration of Tara's visit. She wasn't good, but she *was* tough. Pushing now would only make her retreat.

Tara reached across the tiny café table in the rented kitchen and squeezed Amour's too-thin forearm. "I'll get out of your hair, then. Just give me a minute to put the rest of these groceries away."

Amour glanced at the multiple brown paper bags from the upscale organic market across from the building where Tara worked. "You don't have to do that."

"You're not supposed to exert yourself," Tara tried gently, but Amour got up anyway.

"It's groceries. Believe me, I've handled way worse."

The reality of her words sank into Tara's bones. "How about we split it?" she asked, because screaming at the injustice seemed like a bad option. She'd already put all of the perishables in the fridge when she'd first arrived, anyway.

Amour shrugged. "Sure. Whatever."

Taking on the heavy lifting, Tara pulled the last of the eight grocery bags she'd brought with her to the counter with a *thunk*. Her muscles had given her what-for as she'd loaded the bags onto the rolling cart she'd brought to transport everything to Amour's apartment in one go, then done an encore as she'd done the car to lobby to elevator to doorstep route. She'd had to take a very specific, somewhat circuitous path to make sure the building's security cameras caught her (and anyone who might follow her) every step of the way, but if it kept Amour safe, it would be worth it.

Speaking of which.

"I'm really glad you decided to stick with testifying against Sansone," she said, pulling a can of soup from the bag in front of her and sliding it into a cupboard.

"I don't want to," Amour replied flatly. "But if I don't and the case gets dismissed, he'll probably kill me anyway. He's not the kind of guy who leaves loose ends, you know? The best shot I have at not ending up dead is to testify. Even if I have to stay holed up until then."

Not one to mince words, Tara said, "You're probably right that it's the best way to stay safe in the long run, even though it seems counter-intuitive to testify after what he did. But he threatened you *because* he's scared of you. He only wants you to think he's got the control."

A dismissive noise crossed Amour's lips. "His guy seemed pretty in control when he did all this."

She gestured to her temple, where the mass of gauze had been reduced to a large adhesive bandage covering her wound. But oh, no. *No.* Thoughts like this were going to submarine Amour's strength, and she was going to need all of it to prep for this trial.

"You're still stronger than him."

"You know Detective Garza brought me groceries like, the day I got here, right?" Amour asked, and even though Tara noticed the about-face in subject, she didn't call it out.

"Well, yes, but it doesn't hurt to be prepared with a little extra." Pointing to the bowl Amour had left on the table, she took aim at a grin. "Plus, I bet he didn't bring you any Double Belgian Chocolate Chip."

That got a smile out of her, albeit a small one. "He didn't."

"Okay, then. Now you have all the bases covered." Tara unloaded the rest of the contents from the bag in front of her before saying, "I guess the extra snacks are a little bit of a peace offering, too. I'm sorry I haven't been able to come out before now."

Although Tara had spoken to Amour daily thanks to the secure-line magic Capelli had worked on the phone in the apartment, Sinclair had wanted the dust to settle before he allowed in-person visits from anyone other than the detectives on the case. Even then, those had been limited.

"It's all good," Amour said over a shrug. "I know you're busy working on the trial."

"Yes, but part of that is making sure you're okay, so..."

She trailed off expectantly until Amour had no choice but to respond. "I told you, I'm fine."

Tara's instincts gave up another hearty ping. But before she could put them to words, an oddly patterned knock sounded off on the door.

"Are you expecting anybody?" Tara asked, her heart doing an aerial backflip against her sternum.

"Oh, that's just Xander," Amour said, and funny, Tara's pulse only moved faster.

"How do you know?" And how was Amour already halfway to the door?

"We have a secret knock. He lives, like, a few doors down, so sometimes he comes to say hey. Make sure everything's cool over here. You know. Cop stuff."

Sooooo many things to unpack there. Tara went with safety first. "Let me double-check, just to be sure." Leaning in, she looked through the peephole, and sure enough, Xander stood on the other side just as easy (and hot) as you please, wearing jeans and a snug gray T-shirt and a half-smile that made Tara's libido go full tilt.

"Told you," Amour said. But she smiled as she said it, so Tara simply stepped back and let her open the door just wide enough to let Xander in, then shut it tight behind him.

"Hey, you." Xander lifted a brown paper bag as he greeted Amour. "I thought you might be hungry, so I brought some—oh." His smile did an insta-fade as his gaze landed on Tara and widened. "I'm sorry. I didn't know you had company."

Amour rolled her eyes, although not meanly. "It's okay, it's just Tara. She brought me some groceries and stuff."

"Sinclair said it would be okay if I stopped by now that Amour has been here for a week," Tara ventured. She'd seen Xander in passing at the Thirty-Third precinct over the last five days, but she hadn't had a chance to speak to him one on one since that night at the hospital when he'd calmed her down.

A.K.A, the night she'd stepped so close to him, they could've kissed.

Oh, how she'd wanted that kiss.

"Right," Xander said, and Tara blinked her way back from Fantasy Island. "Well, I just stopped by to drop this off. It's nothing fancy, just a Cuban sandwich." His stare moved over the empty bags just visible in the kitchen thanks to the combination of open concept/small space in the apartment, taking in the gourmet grocery store logo with a frown. "But I see you're already set, so I can just—"

"Are there onion rings in there like last time?" Amour asked, her eyes lighting up as she reached for the bag.

Xander's hesitation lasted for less than a second before he smiled. "Are you kidding me? Of *course* there are. The Crooked Angel's onion rings are practically a religious experience."

Amour took the bag, popping it open and taking a long inhale. "You're pretty cool for a cop. Just saying."

For the first time since before the assault, she looked like herself, her smile carefree and genuinely happy, and it hit Tara right in the center of her chest.

She didn't just look happy.

She looked alive.

"Thanks," Xander said, lifting his chin toward the kitchen. "Go eat before it gets cold. I'll check in on you again tomorrow, when I'm not intruding."

Tara's mouth opened out of pure impulse. "Actually, I was just on my way out, but I'd like to have a word with you privately if I could, Xander? It won't take long."

Surprise flashed through his light green eyes, but he

covered it with a quick, "Sure. My place is right down the hall. If that works?"

"Perfect."

They both said a quick goodbye to Amour and made sure she was securely locked in before Xander pulled his keys out of his pocket and led the way down the hall. He didn't say anything, waiting until they'd crossed the threshold to his apartment—a replica of Amour's in layout —to speak.

"Sorry it's a bit of a mess," he said, looking at the half-empty water bottle and two days' worth of mail on the coffee table and the pair of cross-trainers littering the floor by the couch. Before Tara could tell him it would take more than a little clutter to offend her, he continued. "Anyway, what can I do for you?"

He was so just-business that Tara nearly balked. But what she wanted to say was too important to dismiss, and anyway, she wasn't really a back-down kind of woman. "I wanted to thank you for keeping such a close eye on Amour."

Xander's brows lifted. "That's my job."

"Maybe the surveillance part," Tara conceded, although the partial was all he was going to get out of her. "But the check-ins and takeout food...I haven't seen her brighten up like that since before the assault, and if her over-stocked pantry is anything to go by, you're the only one getting her to eat. So, thank you."

Stuffing his hands in the pockets of his jeans, he said, "It's no big deal," but oh, no. Tara wasn't about to let him slide.

"Could you please say 'you're welcome' so I don't have to keep pushing?" She wrapped just enough humor around the words to lighten them. "I've been in court all day and I'd love the breather."

Bingo. "You're welcome," Xander said with a smile that— whoa—made her want to blush. "So, how was court, by the way? I heard the meeting with the judge the other day was a bust."

Just like that, Tara's good humor faded. "It was what I thought it would be—Sansone's lawyer saying the assault had nothing to do with his client, Sansone providing an alibi, and Judge Waters asking me if I had any evidence linking Sansone to the assault, which I don't. Yet," she added. "But at least now the assault—and my suspicion that Sansone is involved—are both on record. And Judge Waters did agree that keeping Amour's identity hidden was a reasonable precaution. She also warned that if he *is* involved, she won't hesitate to revoke his bail, let my office add to the charges against him, and have him await trial from a prison cell."

"Do you think that will make him more cautious?" Xander asked, but Tara shook her head.

"I think he's got stones the size of Neptune. He knows our case against him hinges on Amour's testimony and he thinks he can scare her into silence because he's a bully. Even if he's backed into a corner, the only thing he'll get is meaner." Tara placed her hands on her hips, her fingers knotting over her navy blue pencil skirt. "But that's fine, because I'll be right here waiting for him when he does."

"You're pretty protective of Amour."

The thought of what could have been—what *had* been all those years ago—jabbed at her throat, making her heart pound faster and the words pour right out of her mouth. "I'm pretty protective of justice being done. Guys like Sansone hurt innocent people. People with families and friends and their whole lives ahead of them. But just like that"—she snapped—"all of that disappears. He wants to *kill* her, Xander, and he's killed who knows how many others. I won't let him get away with that."

For a minute that felt like an hour, or, hell, maybe a month, he looked at her with those wide green eyes that she couldn't read for the life of her. Then, he finally said, "That sounds like a story."

The ball was firmly in her court, Tara knew. She could tell him she was just passionate about her job, which was, oh, by the way, what she'd told everyone who'd ever made the same sort of observation. That's what she *should* do. Telling tough, strong Xander Matthews her story would only make her vulnerable.

So she really had no idea why, when she opened her mouth, the truth started tumbling out.

"When I was nineteen, my best friend, Lucas, and I decided to take a road trip for spring break. It was totally spur of the moment, but he was always coming up with crazy ideas like that."

"Best friend, not boyfriend?" Xander asked, walking to his kitchen like nothing-doing, and Tara followed.

"Yes. His family lived on the same street as mine and his dad and my mom worked for the same medical practice, so we pretty much grew up together. I'm an only child and Lucas was like a brother to me. I know it might sound weird, but I loved having someone who I could be that close with. Someone I could really confide in. He was always there, even on my ugly days. No matter what."

Opening the fridge, Xander slid two bottles of water off the shelf and passed one over to her wordlessly. "I'm tight with my sister. I get it."

Tara nodded. She remembered his sister, Kennedy, from

the case against him that had eventually been dismissed. "Lucas and I both went to Remington University. He was pre-med. He wanted to be a plastic surgeon so he could help kids born with cleft palates and people who'd been hurt in accidents. It was so Lucas—he was just that kind of guy."

"What about you?" Xander led the way to the main living space, his movements as easy as the conversation as he sat down next to her on the couch.

"I was hopelessly undecided," Tara confessed. "My parents wanted me to choose something so I could 'have a career path'. But I was barely nineteen, and I didn't want to choose something for the sake of being able to check a box. I wanted it to be important. Right."

Xander was silent for a minute, his dark brows drawn in a way that told Tara he was processing her words. "That seems smart. I mean, college is expensive. Why waste all that money on something you're not sure of?"

"Or time," Tara said. It had been, as it turned out, the more precious commodity, one that had slipped right through her fingers as uncontrollably as Lucas's blood that night. God, there had been so much blood. Years later, and the dirty, metallic smell of it could still punch her in the back of the throat without warning.

Steeling herself against the tremble that wanted to commandeer her limbs, Tara continued, "Anyway, we'd had a pretty grueling week of midterms that second semester, so Lucas came up with this crazy idea to drive to Miami for spring break. We threw a bunch of clothes in a suitcase and left less than twenty minutes later. The plan was to drive through the night with both of us alternating, then sleep all day on the beach when we got there."

"I take it things didn't go according to the plan," Xander said quietly.

"No." A fragment of dread sliced through her, followed by the ache she knew like a fingerprint. "We'd been on the road for about four hours when we stopped for gas in Sanders Hill, South Carolina."

Xander shook his head, placing his unopened water bottle on the coffee table without his attention straying from her, even for a second. "Never heard of it."

"Not many people have. It's about forty miles from the Georgia state line, population 3,419. No Starbucks. No movie theater. But they do have a 24-hour gas station."

Tara's heart beat faster, adrenaline and fear racing each other in her veins. But she didn't stop. "I went inside with Lucas so I could use the restroom while he grabbed some snacks and paid for the gas. He..." She paused for a breath that did not steady her. "He teased me for being a lightweight and having to go so early in the trip."

Later, on those nights when she couldn't sleep, Tara would replay that moment a million times in her head, wondering how something so small and insignificant could spare her life as it stole her best friend's. "I went into the restroom. I was washing my hands a few minutes later when I heard a loud sound, like a firecracker. Then I heard it two more times in a row, really fast."

"Tara," Xander said, so quietly it could have been a whisper. "You don't have to tell me the rest."

Her eyes burned, but still, she shook her head. Somehow, she *wanted* to tell him, to set the story to words so he'd understand. "I ran out of the restroom just in time to hear the front door slam shut. I didn't understand what had happened—I thought maybe it had been some sort of prank. But then I got to the front of the store, and I saw Lucas on the floor. He'd been shot twice in the chest."

Tara had found out later that the third shot had hit the

woman behind the counter right in the forehead. She'd died instantly.

Lucas hadn't been so lucky.

Tara felt Xander's hand around hers, but she couldn't tell if he'd offered it or she'd sought it out. Either way, she curled her fingers around his and hung on. "There was so much blood. It was everywhere. I remember thinking he was going to be mad because his shirt was ruined. The dumb thing was his favorite." She released a joyless laugh. How utterly stupid she'd been, not to see it. Not to understand that she was the last thing her best friend would ever see. "It didn't occur to me that he would die. Not until he looked at me, anyway, and then, I knew. In all the time I'd known him, I'd never seen Lucas look truly scared. But right then? He was *terrified*."

Two tears tracked down her face, but Xander sat patiently, his hand warm and steady. "I called nine-one-one and pressed my hands over his chest. I told him everything would be okay. I begged him to keep his eyes open, to hang on. When he stopped breathing, I tried to do CPR, but..."

Xander held her hand tighter even though she couldn't say out loud that when she'd tried to do chest compressions and be Lucas's breath, he'd bled harder with every movement. "He coded on the way to the hospital and died before he could get to surgery. The robbery was pretty straightforward, all caught on the gas station's video feeds. The man who did it burst in just after Lucas and I got there. He didn't even hesitate to kill both the clerk and Lucas. It was honestly just a weird twist of fate that I was in the restroom. If he'd known I was, he'd probably have killed me, too."

"I'm so sorry all of that happened to you. And to Lucas," Xander said. "Did they catch the guy?"

"They did." A bitter taste filled Tara's mouth. "But the prosecuting attorneys botched the trial."

"He got *off*?" Xander asked, his jawline going tight.

Not as tight as her rib cage, though. "Yep. He spent sixty-three days in prison waiting for his trial, and then the case was dismissed because the video surveillance footage was thrown out on a technicality." She would never forget the sound of Lucas's mom's cries, deep and guttural with grief as the man who'd killed Lucas had smiled in relief.

Rather than go all awkward on her—or worse yet, throw her a black tie pity party—Xander shocked her by saying, "Shit, Tara. I don't know what to say. That's..."

"Pretty messed up and completely shitty?" she supplied. "Yeah, it is, and it took me a lot of therapy to be able to wrap my head around it."

"Post-traumatic stress is no joke," Xander said, his gaze dropping to the scar on his forearm. An unexpected warmth moved through her chest as she realized he wasn't just being a stand-up guy. He actually *understood*.

And somehow, that made feeling vulnerable in front of him so much easier.

"In a weird way, though, the whole thing ended up being not all bad. After I worked through the initial grief and guilt, I got good and pissed off. I didn't want that kind of injustice to happen to anyone else, so I went to law school and became the best lawyer I possibly could. I treat every case I take on as if it were Lucas's."

"That explains a lot." A wistful expression crossed Xander's face. But before Tara could apologize for how intently she'd pursued the charges against him two years ago, he grabbed her attention with, "So, whatever happened to the guy? Is he still running around free even though he killed two people?"

Ah, at least this part of the story was bittersweet. "Nope. He was stabbed to death in a drug deal that went sideways ten months after the trial. I thought I'd be happy about that —karma, and all. But in the end, it doesn't bring Lucas or that store clerk back. It doesn't make me miss my best friend any less."

Her voice betrayed her lack of calm, but just then, Xander was calm enough for both of them.

"That's definitely true. You can't undo the past. All you can do is move forward one step at a time. But you did that because you're a survivor. You went to law school and became a brilliant lawyer. You fight for people who can't get their own justice. People like Amour. It's pretty badass, when you think about it."

Tara took the words in, her pulse balancing back out and her adrenaline ebbing as she turned them over in her mind. She'd always felt the sting of what she'd lost, the guilt of the twist of fate that had spared her. It had never occurred to her that she was *strong* for having survived.

"I've definitely never thought about it that way," she admitted.

The edges of Xander's mouth lifted, just enough to ease the moment. "You should. You're like a lawyer warrior, doing battle in the name of justice."

Her laugh was soft, but oh, it felt so good. "You did it again, you know."

"Did what?"

"You totally took me out of my head," Tara said. "Just like you did last week, with that duck story."

He tilted his head, his smile still in place. "Guilty as charged. But I knew it was a hard story to tell, just like I knew you were pretty tense the other night."

"It was a really nice thing to do," she said.

Xander shrugged. "Ah, it's no big deal."

"Actually, it *is* a big deal. To me. So, thank you."

"Oh." His lashes swept wide, the dark fringe framing his light green stare. "You're welcome."

In that moment, Tara realized how close their bodies had gotten in the telling of her story. The brush of denim on her bare skin where their knees touched, right at the hemline of her skirt. The warm, steady hold of Xander's hand on hers. The space between her mouth and his that she could eliminate with a simple turn of her body, a lift of her chin that would let her give in to the magnetic pull she'd felt last week in the hospital lobby when she'd wanted nothing more than to kiss him.

Only this time, there was nothing to stop them.

7

I t wasn't until Tara turned and looked at him, her pretty brown eyes darkened with want and her perfect, pink mouth parted just enough to turn his dick to iron, that Xander realized his error.

He knew he could keep control of his desire. Hell, he'd been doing it since the minute he'd set eyes on her smart mouth and sexy curves.

But he hadn't counted on her wanting him *back*.

"You never answered me the other day," Tara said, shifting close enough to make Xander's heartbeat do very strange things. "How come you don't like being called a nice guy?"

"Because I'm not a nice guy."

The answer plowed out of him by default, a truth he knew like a fucking birthright.

Her laugh called him out. "You go out of your way to make sure Amour is okay."

"That's my job," Xander said. "I took an oath to protect people. Just because I take that seriously doesn't mean I'm nice by default."

Unmoved, Tara said, "Okay, then. What about that arson and murder case two years ago? Without your help, a lot of people could've been hurt."

Xander pushed back on the adrenaline that made his heart pound at the reminder. "People were still hurt," he said.

"And *you* didn't hurt them," she countered. He arched a brow at the technicality, which—of course—she returned with an arched brow of her own. "You're still a nice guy."

Christ, she was so close to him, her knee pressed against his and her skirt riding up just high enough to make him want to tear the thing clean off of her. "I'm really not."

"I think you are," Tara insisted, and something inside of him broke.

"And *I* think that if you knew what I was thinking right now, you wouldn't think I'm so nice."

Her chin lifted defiantly, the fire in her eyes taking another jab at his already questionable composure. "Try me."

"Fine," Xander shot back, knowing even as he heard the words that they were the worst sort of idea. "I'm thinking about how badly I want to kiss you. I'm thinking about the sounds that would come out of your mouth if I slid my hand up that sexy little skirt of yours. How hot you'd feel. How wet. But most of all, I'm thinking about how I wouldn't want to stop until you come so hard, you forget everything you know other than my fucking name."

The "oh" that collapsed past her lips was more sigh than word. "Well, then," she breathed, looking up at him from beneath the sweep of her coppery lashes. "If you want it that badly, maybe you should do it."

"Tara." Her name was a warning, low and hot in his throat.

She didn't heed it. "I want this as much as you do, Xander. Please." She moved forward, impossibly close. "Kiss me."

The words were barely out before he'd slanted his mouth over hers. She made a noise of surprise—Christ, that made two of them—but then her arms were around his shoulders, her body pressed against him like a lush, filthy suggestion, and nothing in the world other than a no from her was going to make him stop.

Xander held her face between both palms, his thumbs tracking over the delicate swoop of her cheekbones as he knotted his fingers in her hair and tightened. The sound that came out of her shot directly to his cock, and the next thing he knew, he'd wrecked the tidy twist keeping all that auburn hair in line. Tara parted her lips at his rough demand for entry, but it wasn't to let him take. No, her tongue met his in a purposeful glide, the kiss growing deeper and more needful at the same time. Making him want. Making him need. Waking him up as if he'd been sleepwalking for his entire goddamn life.

She was going to ruin him with nothing more than a kiss, and he was going to love every second.

Sliding one arm around the back of her rib cage, Xander angled her over the couch cushions. Her skirt—God, that fucking *skirt*—didn't allow for much access, and at her sigh of frustration, he reached down low for the hem and yanked it up around her hips.

"Yes," Tara murmured, a sentiment thoroughly echoed by Xander's aching cock as he caught a glimpse of her curvy thighs and the dark blue panties cradling the spot where they met. He moved out of pure instinct, pressing himself over her from chest to hips, saving the barest shred of sanity to offset his weight with one hand on the cushion so he didn't hurt her.

"Oh, *God*, yes," came Tara's honeyed response. She thrust her hips against his, unbearably soft where he was unspeakably hard, fitting against him perfectly.

Xander couldn't decide if she felt like heaven or home, but either way, he never wanted to leave.

He thrust roughly in return. The heat of her pussy sent small shockwaves up his spine even though layers of clothes still separated them, and he did it again out of pure selfishness. Tara answered by arching up as her head fell back, her hair wild and her face flushed with want, her skirt rucked up around her waist as he pushed harder between her legs. Never in a trillion years could Xander have imagined such a sweet sin, and the sight of her knocked into him with palpable force.

He was inches away from ruthlessly fucking her on the secondhand couch he'd inherited from his brother-in-law when instead, she should be treated like a queen.

"Tara." He pulled back, despite the righteously indignant *WTF, man!* coming from his dick. She blinked up at him, her expression catching in worry that made Xander want to kick himself. Hard.

"What's wrong?"

"Christ, nothing." Unable to help himself, he brushed a kiss over her mouth. "You're perfect. It's just..." Tension crowded his muscles, and damn it, had he been insane, losing his composure like that? Tara wasn't the kind of woman he could just screw on impulse, especially after everything she'd just trusted him with. She deserved better than that. "I want to do this right."

A wry smile tilted her lips upward, shocking him clean through. "Trust me, Xander. You are *totally* doing it right."

Her tart comeback pushed a laugh right out of him, scattering his tension like smoke in a spring breeze. "That's not exactly what I meant."

"Okay," Tara said, using the space he'd given her to right her skirt and push herself up to seated beside him. "Talk to me."

Her tone was so devoid of drama or irritation or, hell, anything other than wide open honesty, that his feelings just slid on out.

"How many people have you told about Lucas?"

Tara's brows traveled up in obvious surprise, but Xander didn't backpedal. "Just go with me, here. How many?"

She stayed quiet for a minute, then another, before saying, "Well, my boss knows—it's in my personnel file because of the trial, and my job isn't exactly low-stress. He likes to make sure all of his ADAs are in a good headspace, so we talked about it briefly when I came on board."

"Right, but that was a disclosure thing for work," Xander said, although he was glad her boss seemed like a decent guy.

Tara tilted her head in a non-verbal *fair enough*. "Everyone in college knew about it, but I was too raw to actually talk about it with anyone other than my therapist. I never got too close to any of my friends in law school." Here, her shoulder lifted against the back of the couch in the tiniest shrug. "It's not easy to form deep friendships when you've lost the one that meant the most to you, you know? I told a few of them anyway—by then, I was okay talking about it in a general sense. But it's obviously pretty emotional for me, so...oh." Understanding stole across her face, her eyes sweeping wide. "Is *that* why you stopped? Because I confided in you?"

"Tara, I want to make one thing really clear. I meant

what I said. I want nothing more than to take you to my bedroom, strip off all your clothes, and make you lose your mind a hundred different ways. But between everything that's happened with Amour and what you just laid out, it's been a long week. If we do this"—Xander caught her stare and held—"I don't want it to be some impulsive thing."

"Impulse isn't so bad," she pointed out, but still, he stayed firm.

"It is when it leads to regret."

Tara's brows lifted slightly, the flash in her eyes telling him in no uncertain terms that she was about to argue. "I think I made it pretty clear that I want this."

"You did," Xander said. Sweet Jesus in the manger, she *really* had. "And I want it, too. But I also want to do it right."

Tara looked at him for a heartbeat, then two, then ten. Then, her lips quirked in the makings of a smile. "Can we *please* give up the notion that you're not a nice guy?"

Xander laughed softly. "You're not going to let that one go, are you?"

"Not even for a second. But it just so happens that I argue with people for a living, so I'm all too happy to prove it to you if that's what it takes. Now, do you want to grab some dinner? Woman cannot live on ice cream alone."

XANDER LOOKED up at the building in front of him and immediately started to sweat. Apart from an elementary school field trip to the Remington Fine Arts Museum, he'd never seen this much marble in one place. A dark red awning led to a set of brass-lined double doors, complete with a uniformed doorman on the other side, ready and waiting with a smile or an umbrella or whatever else the residents might need.

"Good evening, sir," the man said as he ushered Xander all the way into the lobby, and Xander had to fight the urge to turn around to see who the guy was really talking to. "How may I help you this evening?"

Surreptitiously brushing off the rain that had dampened his jacket on the two-block hustle from his car to the building, Xander said, "Oh. I'm, uh, here to see Tara Kingston."

Holy shit, the lobby had a chandelier. No, wait—*two* of them. And here he was, in his favorite worn-in canvas jacket and equally banged-up boots, carrying a big bag of takeout food from The Crooked Angel like a goddamn delivery service.

This was a fucking mistake.

"Ms. Kingston, of course." The doorman smiled, and okay, he didn't seem ready to toss Xander on his ass or anything. "Mr. Matthews, then?"

Xander's brows lifted. "Yes, sir."

"She's expecting you." At what had to be the totally bewildered look on Xander's face, he added, "She called down to say you'd be arriving shortly. The elevator to the East Tower is through the lobby and to the right. Have a nice night."

"Great. Thanks." Having memorized the apartment number Tara had texted him this morning when she'd invited him over for dinner, Xander made his way to the elevator. The elegantly mirrored car gave him a chance to smooth a hand over his jeans and make sure his T-shirt was still as clean as when he'd shouldered into it in the locker room at the Thirty-Third. The elevator chimed its arrival on the eleventh floor, the doors gliding open to reveal a hallway that was just as upscale as the rest of the building, and he followed it to the door marked *1104* in oiled bronze numbers.

Tara answered his knock after only a few seconds, erasing all of Xander's unease with one smile. "Hey! You made it."

He crossed the threshold and nodded. "I did. This place is"—he took in the hand-scraped hardwood floors, the light, open living space that was the size of a gymnasium, yet somehow still managed to be cozy, and the stacked stone fireplace taking over the far wall—"wow."

"You like it?" Tara asked brightly. "After we eat, I'll give you the full tour. But first..." She pressed up to the balls of her bare feet, her mouth warm and sweet as she placed a quick peck on his jaw. "Thank you for bringing dinner."

"It's no big deal," he said, wondering how the fuck he'd managed to grit his way through his Physical Ability Tests at the police academy just fine, yet he was pretty sure he'd just been felled by a two-second kiss from a five foot five redhead.

Tara tipped back her head and laughed, not making Xander's situation any easier. "I beg to differ. According to Amour, these onion rings are going to make me see God. That is a *very* big deal." She took the bag from his hand, gesturing toward an L-shaped sectional sofa with a nod before leading the way. "And anyway, bringing dinner was a really nice thing to do. Do you want to do the honors while I grab us something to drink? I've got water, soda, beer, wine..."

"Beer works. Thank you," he said. He had a rare day off tomorrow, although he'd likely spend a lot of it reviewing the case. If he stuck to one and then watered up afterward, he'd be fine to drive.

"You got it."

She returned just as Xander had finished unloading everything, a beer in each hand, and his chin lifted in surprise.

"What?" Tara asked, passing one of the beers over as she took a sip from the other.

He might not have known her for that long in the grander scheme of the universe, but he knew better than to go the *nothing* route with her. "I just didn't take you for a beer drinker. Or a jeans and sweatshirt wearer, to be honest," he said, although, damn, the way her soft pink top slid just far enough off her shoulder to give him All The Bad Ideas was more than a little hot.

"What, you think I hang out at home in my suit and heels, drinking Cristal and eating caviar?" Her laughter softened any heat the words might've otherwise carried, making it all too easy for Xander to laugh, too.

"Maybe not that extreme. But we've spent every evening this week together, and you've never *not* been in a suit," he pointed out.

"Every evening this week I came to your building directly from work. I'm not *all* business."

"You're mostly business," Xander said, partly because it was true and partly because the fire that sparked in her eyes whenever he messed with her was too hot to pass up.

Tara didn't disappoint. "Yet here I am, enjoying a beer in my favorite pair of jeans—which have a hole in them and everything"—she paused to point dramatically to her knee, coppery brows lifted as if to say *Exhibit A, Your Honor*—"so maybe I'm just a regular girl after all."

It took all Xander had not to laugh his head clean off at that. "Well, I hope you're a *hungry* regular girl."

"Starving," she admitted, settling cross-legged on the floor in front of the coffee table. "Okay. What've we got?"

"Well, you said to bring you the best thing on the menu, so in order to give you the full Crooked Angel experience, I kind of had to get creative." Starting to open up the cartons, he said, "For appetizers, we've got Tex-Mex eggrolls, calamari with cilantro aioli, and homemade Pierogis. For the main course, I'd be doing you wrong if I didn't bring a Cuban—they're the restaurant's signature sandwich—but the shrimp tacos are ridiculous, too, and this pesto chicken sandwich is new, so I thought we'd give it a go. Oh, and obviously"—Xander popped the lid on the last container, his mouth going all Pavlov—"plenty of onion rings."

Tara scanned the coffee table, taking it all in. "I have a feeling I'm going to wish I'd worn my favorite leggings instead of my favorite jeans, but okay. Let's do this."

After a half dozen pieces of calamari and two bites of an eggroll, Xander realized he was going to have a kickstand in his jeans for the duration of the evening. "Oh, my God," Tara moaned blissfully, popping the last of her eggroll past her sweet, sinful lips. "I want to eat these every day. So...*good*."

Xander swooped up a Pierogi with his plastic fork and smiled. "Kennedy would be happy to hear you say that. Although, I don't know, maybe now you'd make her cry."

"Yikes. That sounds extreme," Tara said at the same time Xander realized his mis-step.

But there was no going back now, so he said, "Yeah. She just found out she's having a baby, so I guess the crying is a thing. But I'm not supposed to tell anyone the happy news yet, so..."

She mimed zipping her lips and tossing away the key. "I'm a vault. Still, that's pretty exciting, right?"

"Yeah," Xander said, taking a few more bites before adding, "She pretty much raised me, so we're closer than most siblings. She's worked really hard." It was the world's most colossal understatement for what Kennedy had done, all she'd sacrificed, much of it for him. But the curiosity in Tara's eyes might as well be burning a hole in him right now, so he pulled on the cover of a shrug. "She and Gamble are happy. They're going to be kickass parents, and I get to be the fun uncle who buys the drum set. It's all good."

"I don't really know a lot of people who have gotten to the point in their lives where they decide whether or not they want to have kids," Tara said thoughtfully, and here, Xander could relate. "Then again, I don't really have many close friends, and even though I'm pretty tight with my parents, our family is basically just the three of us."

Now Xander's curiosity sparked. "What about work? You're not close with anyone there?"

Tara shook her head. "Nah. The other A.D.A.s are all pretty much workaholics, like me. Which isn't entirely a bad thing when you love your job, but it doesn't exactly lead to a chummy environment."

"It could, though," Xander speculated. "I mean, I kind of fell into this great, big extended family when my sister married Gamble. Those firefighters work their asses off. The cops at the Thirty-Third, too. But they're also unbelievably tight. Aside from me and Kennedy, they're the only family Gamble even has."

"Really?" Tara's fork stopped mid-air, her brown eyes wide. "There have to be, what, ten first responders at Station Seventeen? Twelve? And you're close with *all* of them?"

Xander had no shortage of fondness for everyone in the group, despite his rocky introduction to all of them, including his brother-in-law. "Oh, yeah. The docs at

Remington Mem, too. We all hang out a couple times a week, mostly at The Crooked Angel, but some of us do other stuff. Gamble and I play basketball once a week with Isabella's husband, Kellan, and his buddy, Devon. We all kind of group together for barbecues in the summer and most holidays. Oh, and we always hang out for hockey playoffs," he added. "Kennedy's best friend, January? She's married to Finn Donnelly, so it's pretty much law that we all watch the games together to cheer him on."

"You know Finn *Donnelly*," Tara said slowly. "The star forward for the Charlotte Rogues."

"Yep. Cool guy. He hosts a killer fundraiser at The Crooked Angel every year."

"Wow." Tara took a long sip from her beer bottle, the look on her face wistful enough to make his heart take a stutter-step in Xander's chest. "I can't imagine what it's like to be part of such a big group of people who are all so close. To be honest, the thought of it is a little scary to me."

"Scary how?" Xander asked.

"It's an awful lot of people to let in. I guess I'm just kind of guarded because of my past."

Hell if he didn't know all the words to *that* song. Not that he could tell her that. Christ, if she knew even half of what he'd done in his past, she'd probably regret trusting him with her dinner preferences, let alone some of the most emotional parts of her personal history.

And still, that didn't stop him from wanting her to, because that was the sort of bastard he was. "You could try starting with just one person," he said. "Maybe then it wouldn't be so scary."

Tara's smile made his chest squeeze. "I think I'd actually really like that."

And as they spent the next three hours talking and laughing and losing track of every single thing around them that wasn't each other, Xander realized he didn't just want Tara to trust him.

He wanted to trust her, too.

8

Tara pulled into a parking spot a block from the Thirty-Third Precinct and grinned at her good luck. Okay, so it was a bazillion degrees out, and yeah, she'd have to walk that block pretty quickly—in three-inch heels, no less—if she was going to make her meeting with Isabella and the Intelligence Unit. But despite working some breakneck hours to manage both her normal caseload and the trial prep for the Sansone case, she'd been able to spend the last four evenings in a row with Xander, hence her inclination to smile both randomly and often.

He'd surprised her by having a sense of humor nearly as dry as her own, along with a love for Renaissance history and the ability to make a killer dirty martini. He *hadn't* surprised her by being smart or pretty quiet about super personal stuff unless nudged, but Tara wasn't exactly a stranger to guiding conversations. While Xander had remained pretty tight-lipped about some of his past, he'd also told her no less than four dozen stories about his sister, Kennedy, her husband, Gamble, and the rest of the fire-fighters from Station Seventeen that served as his found family. Although she'd loved listening to Xander go on about his sister and all of their close friends, Tara couldn't deny the odd ache she'd felt in her chest as she'd listened to him talk.

What would it be like to be close with people like that? To trust that they'd always be there for her? That they'd never leave?

The way she was starting to trust Xander, and God, she didn't hate it.

"Oh, stop," Tara chided herself, replacing the smile that had faded from her lips with a newer, if less comfortable, version. Yes, she was enjoying the time she and Xander spent together, and *oh* yes, she'd definitely enjoyed the steamy goodnight kisses they'd traded over the past week and a half, ever since that first one at his place the night he'd brought Amour dinner. But the thought of belonging with anyone like that? Of being cared for at that level? That deeply?

She might as well be wishing for rainbows *and* unicorns, with quadruple orgasms on top.

Straightening her shoulders beneath her suit jacket, she scooped up her purse and got out of her car. The walk was as short and hell-hot as expected, and by the time she'd made her way through the lobby, then the metal detectors and security check-in that allowed access to the Intelligence Unit's offices, Tara was fully focused on the case at hand.

"Hey! If it isn't my favorite A.D.A.," came Isabella's welcoming voice from the midway point in the large, open-concept main office space. Tara had always marveled at how the Intelligence Unit worked as a true team—no cubicles for this crew. The only private rooms were Sergeant Sinclair's office and the interrogation rooms along the back hallway of the space.

"I bet you say that to all the A.D.A.s," Tara said, her smile hanging in her voice.

Capelli looked up from the bank of monitors spanning half of the far wall of the office, pushing his black-framed glasses up over his nose. "Actually, she doesn't. Most of us really do like you best."

Tara had to laugh at how forthright the guy always was. "Most of you?"

"Well, Garza doesn't seem to have a preference," Capelli mused. "But I wouldn't take that personally. His gruff demeanor dictates that he doesn't really have a preference for anyone."

Isabella's partner, Liam Hollister, let out a thinly disguised laugh-cough from his spot at the desk across from her, as Garza—who was sitting well within earshot of the entire conversation—sent a hard look at Capelli.

"I can *hear* you, Wikipedia."

Yikes. Tara had seen sweeter expressions from defense attorneys on critical cross-examinations.

Capelli, however? Seemed unfazed. "I'm well aware of your keen sense of hearing, Detective. My commentary on your demeanor was purely observational. No offense intended."

"You've gotta admit, he's not wrong, G," Hollister said, his grin expanding as Garza's expression remained...well, gruff.

"Yeah, yeah," Garza grunted, although the words—and his frown—seemed to have lost their bite. He aimed his dark gaze at Tara. "Anyway, what's the word on Sansone?"

Ugh. "I was hoping you guys could tell me."

Isabella frowned, then nodded at Capelli, who brought the digital case board to life on a large, wall-mounted screen at the back of the office. "Unfortunately, not much. Hollister and Garza and Dade recanvassed Amour's neighborhood and got a whole lot of nothing on her attacker."

"Xander mentioned that when I saw him the other night," Tara said, matching Isabella's frown. She hadn't been expecting much, but... "How about the forensics from the crime scene?"

"We just got the last of the reports back from the lab this morning," Capelli said, motioning to the monitor. *Do not look at the photographs of Amour's injury. Do not look—*

Tara moved her gaze to focus on the images of Amour's house, staring hard. "Anything there?"

"Unfortunately, no," Capelli said. "No prints that don't belong to Amour or the handful of friends she said visited in the few weeks before the assault. We checked for hair and fiber even though I know I don't have to tell you that finding either isn't exactly definitive without other evidence."

No, he really didn't. Tara couldn't even count how many times she'd heard the story of the forensics investigator who had found a hair at the scene of a double-homicide that detectives had thought would break the case wide open... only to have the DNA match that of the detective's wife. Poor guy had unknowingly brought it into the crime scene on his jacket, and the story had become the stuff of defense attorneys' wildest dreams. "Yes, I'm well aware. I take it we didn't find any, regardless?"

"No." Isabella sighed. "We did get a partial boot print in the dirt outside that's a little promising. We can't be sure it doesn't belong to a meter reader or a delivery person, but we do know the wearer is a big guy."

"Size fifteen, to be exact," Hollister put in, and okay, that they could work with.

"So, it could definitely belong to our assailant. Anything

specific about the brand?" Tara asked, hope perking in her chest.

It sputtered out a second later. "Second most popular in the U.S.," Capelli said, clicking over to a photograph. "Available on dozens of online sites as well as five hundred fifty-two different stores all over the country."

"Shit," Tara muttered.

"My feelings exactly." Garza folded his arms over his chest, his shoulder holster hugging a set of muscles that made him almost as menacing as his dark stare. "I'd love nothing more than to nail this asshole and get him *and* Sansone off the streets."

"How about the tattoo?" Tara asked, but Capelli shook his head.

"There are tens of thousands of tattoos in our database, and those are just the ones we have record of. The hash mark detail does narrow it down a bit, but it's still a popular design, and she didn't recognize it, which means it's likely her attacker doesn't work at the club."

Damn it. "So, we can't narrow it down."

"No." Hollister shook his head. "Sansone has a few guys on his club payroll who are big enough to fit the size description, but they're either not white or not inked that we can tell."

Tara bit back her frustration. "Which means all we really have to go on is this tattoo."

Capelli nodded, although he looked far from happy about the affirmative. "Statistically speaking, the odds of finding the man who assaulted Amour on a partial of a tattoo that she only got a glimpse of one time under duress are exceedingly improbable."

"And even if we do, we'll still have to tie him to Sansone," Hollister said, running a hand through his red-brown hair. "Guys like that don't exactly get chatty. Not when they know what douchebags like Sansone are capable of."

"I take it he's been a Boy Scout this week." Tara didn't even bother trying to keep her disdain from seeping into her tone.

Capelli turned away from the case board. "Maxwell and Hale are doing surveillance on his club as we speak. Nothing much there, though. He's only come in a few times since the assault. He stays for a few hours, then heads for home."

"He's lying low, just like we thought he would," Isabella said. "But he's clearly desperate not to go to trial, otherwise he never would've risked threatening Amour in the first place, and he knows by now that his threat didn't work."

"He should," Tara agreed. Her only spark of hope right now was that Sansone would get desperate at the realization and slip up. "The trial date is set, and Amour is still on the witness list." She'd be protected, of course, since she was acting as an informant, and her testimony would be given via closed-circuit video, with her face and voice disguised. "His attorney is a sleazebag, but he's not stupid. He knows that Amour is my key witness. He also knows that if she was refusing to testify, I'd have reached out to try to cut a deal."

Isabella nodded, one hand absently rubbing her belly. "And she's doing okay?"

"She's as well as she can be, under the circumstances." In truth, Xander was the only person who could get her anywhere close to a smile, and even that was hit or miss.

"I've got some possibles from the tattoo database for her to look at," Capelli said. "I'm not sure they'll amount to anything, but one of the detectives can bring them out to review them with her."

"I can go this afternoon," Isabella volunteered.

"Great," Tara said, mentally going over her schedule for the rest of the day. "Let me know when you're going? I'd like to be there with her when she looks over them, as long as that's okay with you?"

"Of course. Why don't I walk you downstairs and we can work out the details?"

After a handful of goodbyes to the rest of the Intelligence Unit, Tara shouldered her bag and fell into step beside Isabella.

"I hate that I can't be on the protection detail for this one," Isabella grumbled, but Tara shook her head.

"All the case work is important. It's probably how we're going to catch whoever hurt Amour and I'll need an airtight case to bring the guy in, so you're helping plenty. Plus"—she smiled—"you're already kind of on protection detail with this little..."

"Guy." Isabella beamed.

"Oh, a boy! That's really exciting."

They rounded the corner to the precinct lobby, and if Isabella answered her, Tara couldn't have said. Because Xander stood at the sergeant's desk, his light green stare intent as he listened to something his partner was telling him, his patrol uniform outlining all of his lean muscles and the hard angles of his body just enough to suggest what they'd feel like if he pulled her close, and holy hell, how was it suddenly a million degrees in here?

"Oh, but that's *more* exciting," Isabella murmured, calling Tara out with her grin.

"I, uh." *Eloquent. Real smooth.* Oh, screw this. "Yeah. It might be kind of exciting? But it's not affecting the case at all," Tara added, worry crowding her chest. "I assure you, keeping Amour safe is our first priority."

"What you do on your own time is entirely your business." Isabella lifted her hands. "I know you're a good lawyer, just like I know Xander's a good cop. You're not breaking any rules, and neither one of you would ever jeopardize a case."

As if he'd heard his name across the noisy lobby, Xander looked up, his gaze catching Tara's and his mouth tugging up into a smile that moved all the way through her. Her cheeks heated in the best possible way, and she lifted a hand in a small wave.

Tilting her head, Isabella surprised Tara by asking, "Can I give you a word of advice, friend to friend?"

"Oh." A pang hit her belly at the word *friend*. "I, ah. Sure?"

"Xander is a great guy, but he's not without ghosts. Do yourself a favor." Isabella's smile grew kind. "If you like him as much as your face says you do, don't let him hide from you. Because if he likes you as much as *his* face says he does, he's going to try."

Tara blinked. Granted, less than three weeks had passed since he'd calmed her in that hospital lobby, but they'd been filled with a fast sort of closeness, an unspoken certainty that felt to Tara an awful lot like trust. "You think he's going to hide from me?"

"I think he might not know how not to hide some things," Isabella said. "He had a rough life before he became a cop. Sometimes the past dies hard."

Well, shit. She'd already sensed Xander holding back a part of himself, and she *was* pretty well acquainted with how that worked, now wasn't she? Speaking of which...

"Sounds like you're speaking from experience." Hearing the directness of the impulsive thought she'd put to words, Tara's cheeks prickled. "I apologize. That was—"

"Accurate," Isabella finished. Her smile didn't budge; if anything, it strengthened. "Which is exactly why I'm giving you this advice. I've been there before, too. I'm not suggesting you push him—if he's not ready to talk, he won't. But I have a feeling he wants to trust you. He might just need you to show him that he can."

Looking across the lobby at Xander, Tara realized two things. One was that she *did* like him as much as Isabella had noticed. Maybe more.

The other was that she wanted him to trust her with his ghosts. No matter how scary they might be.

9

Xander knew he should be focused on whatever Dade was telling him, and in his defense, he'd put his back into the effort. But—also in his defense, thank you very much—Tara was wearing another one of those slim skirts that made his composure want to spontaneously combust, and when she'd locked eyes with him from across the lobby and smiled, the rest of the room, the rest of the city; hell, the rest of the universe didn't matter.

In that moment, she was the only person in the world.

Also, she was headed directly for him.

"Hey," Xander said, suddenly wishing he'd done better than the *fuck it, good enough* route with his hairbrush this morning. "I didn't expect to see you here today."

"I had a quick meeting with Isabella and the team. I figured you'd be out on patrol, otherwise I'd have mentioned it last night," Tara said, smiling at him before turning toward Dade. "It's nice to see you again, Officer Dade."

"Glad it's under better circumstances this time," Dade

replied, her tone strangely devoid of its trademark sarcasm. "You going to throw the book at the son of a bitch who hurt that poor girl?"

"Yes, ma'am, I most certainly am," Tara promised. "Speaking of which"—she returned her attention to Xander, and yeah, he felt it everywhere—"Isabella and I are going to meet up later to go over some images on the tattoo database with Amour. Do you want to meet me there?"

Xander nodded. "Absolutely. I promised her I'd check in after my shift, anyway."

"I know she'll be happy to see you, and if you're there when she reviews the photo arrays, it saves me from having to get you up to speed later. I'll text you when I leave the office?"

"Sure, that sounds great."

"Okay, it's a date. You two stay safe out there," she said, giving up one last smile before she turned toward the front door. She'd barely made it out of earshot before Dade pounced.

"You'd better start talking, Matthews. And do *not* insult me by asking 'about what?'."

Ah, hell. Xander should've known she wouldn't have missed the look he and Tara had traded, crowded lobby or no. But his defenses weren't about to let him get all gabby about it.

Not that Dade was going to let him out from under the microscope unless he played this just right. He tested the water with, "I'm not sure what you want me to say."

One black brow arched. "Well, let's start with you working this case. The Intelligence Unit doesn't usually ask patrol officers for a whole lot of assistance after a canvas is done."

Okaaaay, not the path he'd expected her to take, but... "It

was blind luck that Amour trusted me that night in the hospital. She could've just as easily shut down, and then Sinclair would have sent me right back here, where I belong."

"You've been a cop for how long, and you're still over there believing in blind luck? Please." Dade snorted. "Do you know the last cop Sinclair plucked off patrol for help with 'just one case'?"

"No," Xander said.

Of course, Dade did. "It was Hale."

Okay, whoa. Addison Hale was one of Intelligence's brightest and most badass. Not that there were any slackers up there, but still. "I'm not *that* good."

"Dear Lord in heaven, please give me patience with this one," Dade muttered, shaking her head as she looked up at the lobby ceiling. "Do you think Sinclair is a dumbass?"

Xander coughed out a laugh that was more surprise than anything else. "God, no." Around the Thirty-Third, even hinting at it was blasphemy.

"Then it's safe to say you don't think he suffers any fools, especially when it comes to the people who work his cases?"

Shit. He'd waltzed right into that one. "I'm telling you, this is a one-time thing."

"Alright, then," Dade said, seeming all too happy to switch gears. "What about that?"

Her gesture to the door that Tara had exited through a few minutes prior made feigning innocence impossible.

"That's kind of complicated," Xander hedged.

"But you like her," Dade pressed.

Xander used all of his energy not to squirm. "Maybe."

A less than polite noise crossed Dade's lips. "Do you know how long I've been a cop? Can we dispense with the bullshit for the sake of not insulting me, please?"

"Okay, yes, I like her," he said, and funny, the words felt better than they should coming out of his mouth. "She's brilliant and fierce and funny and beautiful...and totally out of my league."

Dade's smile was strangely at odds with her sigh. "You know, for a smart man, you are awfully stupid."

"Okaaaay?" Xander stammered, but Dade just laughed.

"Did you miss the way she spoke to you about the case you're working on?"

UNTITLED

He frowned in confusion. "No."

"Then you heard her treat you with equality and respect," Dade led, and okay, so she did have a point.

"I suppose."

"Mmm hmm. And has she ever given you any indication that *she* thinks she's out of your league?"

"Well, no," Xander said carefully. Not since her office had tried to bring charges against him two years ago, but now that he knew *why* she was so dedicated? He couldn't exactly blame her for doing her job, and anyway, he'd earned those charges, fair and fucking square.

"And *please* do not tell me you didn't see the way she looked at you like she wants to have you for Sunday supper," Dade continued, both brows lifted and her hands on her hips, and Xander's shock left him by way of a strangled exhale.

"Dade," he managed, but she shook her head.

"Don't you *Dade* me when you know I'm right," she chided. "That moony face you made when you saw that woman makes it damn clear you've got it bad for her, and anyone with half a mind can see the feeling is mutual. Now, do yourself a favor, Xander Matthews. Get out of your own way and let her like you."

Xander wanted to argue—God, it was *right there* on the tip of his tongue. Yes, the nights he'd spent with Tara over the past week and a half, talking and laughing and kissing, had been some of the best he'd had in...well, he didn't even know how long. But she had an Ivy League law degree that matched her Ivy League life. She deserved more than a former criminal whose only degree was in Advanced Survival from the shittiest part of Remington, even if he had put that part of his life behind him.

Somehow, though, the argument rang hollow in his head. He *had* put that part of his life behind him, and he'd busted his ass for two years to do it. He wasn't perfect. He had the literal scars to prove it. But not only did Tara not seem to care, she also seemed to really like him, just as he was. *Because* of who he was.

So Xander had no choice but to look at Dade and offer up a smile and say what he always did.

"Yes, ma'am."

"Well, *that* didn't go the way I'd hoped."

Tara sat back on Xander's couch and tried to find a silver lining from the ninety minutes they'd spent looking through photo after photo with Amour, only to have the poor girl come up apologetically empty.

Nope. There was no way around it. She'd been hoping for a slam-dunk, and the fact that they hadn't even come close? Flat-out sucked.

As if he'd zeroed in on her thoughts, Xander said, "I

know this sucks. But we knew getting a hit off that tattoo was a long shot, and the case against Sansone is still strong. The closer we get to the trial, the more he'll realize he's in trouble because he hasn't scared Amour from testifying. He'll get desperate and screw up. And when he does, we'll be there to take him down."

"And if he doesn't?" It was a risk, tempting Sansone into brashness—not to mention dangerous. But the Intelligence Unit had Amour under no less than a dozen safeguards, and half the time, Xander was literally down the hall from her on top of that. The chances that Sansone would find her, let alone hurt her and get away with it, were practically nil.

Weren't they?

Xander scooped up Tara's hand, his warm, steady presence instantly loosening the tension in her shoulders. "If he doesn't, then you'll roast him in court with Amour's testimony. Either way, he goes to jail for a really long time."

"How do you do that?" she asked, little shivers moving through her as he skated his thumb over the soft spot where her index finger met her palm.

"Do what?"

"You make it so easy for me to breathe," Tara said, capping the words with a soft laugh. "That sounded a lot less weird in my head. But you always seem to know exactly what I need."

The honesty of it hit her right in the chest, turning those shivers into pure want, and she slid closer to him. "In fact, I'll bet you know what I need right now."

Xander's pupils flared, turning his stare dark. "Tara."

"It's you," she said, because she knew he'd need the words. "You said you wanted to do this right. And this"—Tara leaned in to brush her mouth over his, lingering just long enough to capture his exhale with her smile—"you and me, right now? Doesn't just feel right. It feels perfect. So, please, Xander. Give me what I need. Let me have *you*."

They tangled together in an instant, his hands in her hair and her arms around the beautiful bulk of his shoulders. Xander didn't kiss her gently, and she didn't want him to. One slide of his tongue had her opening readily, giving him full access. They shared control, though, with her answering every taste and every stroke, building the intensity of the kiss. Tara sent up a prayer of thanks that she'd stopped by her apartment to change into a pair of jeans and a tank top, and she used the much easier maneuverability to her advantage as she pressed forward, hooking one knee around Xander's hip and pushing his shoulder blades against the center of the couch.

"There," she murmured against his mouth. "That's better."

Xander gripped her hips, settling her directly over his lap. There was no missing the distinct and—*ohhh, God, yes*—rather sizeable length of his cock notched against the seam of her jeans, and they both moaned in unison at the contact.

"Fuck, Tara." His mouth found her neck, stringing hot, greedy kisses there that made her pulse trip. Vaguely, Tara realized she should probably try for at least *some* decorum. But then Xander lifted one hand to skim his knuckles over her nipple, and screw decorum.

She wanted his fingers. His mouth. His cock, pressing deep inside of her, filling her up and making her scream.

She wanted fucking *everything* from this man.

Tara arched into Xander's touch, one hand on his shoulder, the other lower, over his opposite bicep.

A wicked glint moved through his eyes as he pulled back

to look at her, and oh, the dark and dirty look only made her want him more. "You like that?"

"Yes," she said on a breath that turned into a gasp when he grazed her nipple again.

The glint intensified. "You want more, though. Don't you?"

"Yes." Tara thrust against him, her knees locked over either side of his hips. The friction sent need throbbing through her that doubled in intensity when his knuckles made one more pass over her nipple, now clearly visible against the thin cotton of both her bra and her tank top.

"You want me to take this off you," he said, his certainty keeping the words from becoming a question as he hooked his fingers beneath the hem of her tank top. Not trusting her voice, Tara nodded.

The tank top hit the floor less than a second later. Her nipples were hard points against the pale pink cotton, and Xander bit out a curse that sounded like a benediction.

"Christ. You're so goddamn pretty." He looked nearly awestruck, his gaze on her practically reverent, and Tara's heart raced even harder.

"I want to show you more." Sliding from his lap, she took only enough time to unbutton her jeans and lower them over her hips, then her thighs, then finally kick free of them. She returned to Xander's lap, giving him a full view despite the closeness of their bodies.

His hands circled her rib cage, guiding her into a motion she wanted desperately to find. "You want me to touch you." One thumb edged higher, to the front closure of her bra. *Yes. Yes.* She rocked harder against his cock, warmth filling the spot between her legs.

"You want me to suck your perfect tits." His mouth was so close to her nipple that Tara could feel the heat of his breath, and holy shit, she was going to explode if he didn't touch her.

One palm coasted lower, fingers splayed over her hip as his thumb slipped just beneath the edge of her panties. "You want me to make you come, just like I promised you I would that first night."

It hit her in that moment that he wasn't just talking dirty for the sake of turning her on, even though, sweet Jesus, it was working. No, even though he'd been able to read her like a billboard from the minute they'd met, and she'd given him every indication with her body language that she wanted everything he'd promised and more, Xander was still asking for permission. To touch her. To taste her. To make her come so hard, she forgot everything she knew but his name.

Tara didn't hesitate. "Yes," she said. Covering his hand with hers, she moved it to the clasp of her bra. "Yes. I want all of that. I want all of *you*. And I don't want to wait."

One turn of his wrist had her bra open, another sweep had the thing off her shoulders entirely. Replacing one hand over her hip, he cupped her breast with his opposite hand, holding her steady as his lips closed over her nipple.

"*Oh* my God," Tara cried, sensation ricocheting through her. Using his hand on her hip, Xander guided her back into motion, and even through his jeans, his cock felt like heaven and sin all wrapped up together.

His fingers inched farther beneath her panties, making her pussy clench with need. She lifted up slightly, just enough to give him both space and permission.

He took both.

With one deft movement, he found her center, two fingers sliding home.

"So tight," Xander grated, his face flushed with uncut lust. "Jesus, Tara. You feel so fucking good."

Need sparked in her belly, demanding and hot, and she chased it with a thrust. Xander returned his attention to her nipple, his lips creating just enough pressure to make her breath go tight in her throat. Between the firm pull of his mouth above and the steady push of his fingers below, her need became a full-on scream. In time with her thrusts, he flipped his hand, burying his thumb over her aching clit. Release built like a hurricane inside of her, far from slow or sweet. Xander dared her closer with every wicked touch, and Tara gripped his shoulder, her breath spilling out in needful bursts.

"Take it, baby." He stilled his thumb over her clit, letting her movements against his hand dictate the movement and pressure, and there, there, oh fuck, right...*there*. "Let me be what you need."

Her orgasm pulsed through her, greedy and bright. She rode out every wave, weightless with pure pleasure, until her body and breath began to reset. Xander eased his touches, scaling back and eventually shifting his arms around her rib cage. The desire in his eyes still held a question, and Tara nodded, as sure as she'd ever been of anything.

He shifted his weight, keeping her close as he found his feet and walked them both down the hallway. Placing her on his neatly made bed, he stepped back, tugging his shirt over his head and his jeans over the lean muscles of his hips and legs, leaving only his boxer briefs in place before joining her on the bed.

"Wait," Tara said. Immediately, he stilled, but she shook her head to reassure him. "I'm just going to need a minute with all of"—she gestured to his seriously beautiful body and grinned—"this, please."

"You can take whatever you want," Xander said, turning toward her so she could do exactly that. Setting her hands on his shoulders, she mapped his body with her fingers. Lean muscles. Hard planes. Warm skin. Tara took it all in, half hypnotized and fully turned on.

Only when she got to the scar on his forearm did he flinch ever so slightly. She looked at him in the soft light spilling in from the hallway, her voice as steady as her touch as she said, "I want all of you, Xander. No matter what."

For a second, he didn't speak or move, his expression unreadable in the shadows. But then he nodded, allowing Tara to continue. She stroked her fingers over the scar, smooth in some places, puckered in others. But she never faltered, letting her hands roam over his arms, his chest, down the muscled plane of his abs. The trail of dark hair leading down from his navel rasped against the pads of her fingers, the need in her belly jolting back to life as she slid past the waistband of his boxer briefs to wrap her hand around his cock.

Xander sent her name through his teeth with a hiss. Using her free hand, she undressed him completely, using the freedom of motion to find a steady rhythm. A moan tore from his throat, and he thrust into the circle of her fingers to meet every stroke. Wetness bloomed between her legs at the sight of his pleasure, and she widened her knees to try and offset the emptiness she felt there.

Watching her, he pulled back with a curse. "I need to be inside you," he said. "Right now."

Yes. She must've said the word out loud—or, God, maybe he was just that in sync with her—because he moved to his bedside table to (hallelujah) grab a condom and put it on as quickly as he could while still getting the job done properly. Tara used the opportunity to slip out of her panties, letting her knees fall open so Xander could fit between them as she eased all the way back over his bed. He filled her with one long thrust, their bodies completely joined before they both went still.

"*Ah*," Tara cut out, less word than sound. Xander pressed his forehead over hers, one hand by her shoulder and the other bracketed over her hip. She tried to process all the sensations slamming through her—the pleasure-pain of the fullness between her legs, the heat of Xander's body locked over hers from chest to belly to hips, the sharp intake of his breath.

And then he began to move, and Tara couldn't think.

All she could do was *feel*.

Xander pulled back, only an inch before reclaiming the space he'd created. "Perfect. Christ, Tara, you are..." He punctuated the sentence with another thrust. Her pussy was so slick that he moved with ease despite the tight fit. They found a rhythm in seconds, a flawless back and forth that sent pleasure curling down her spine. Xander stayed steady —God, he was always so steady—with his hand on her hip, guiding her exactly where she wanted to be as he fucked her in hard, slow thrusts. Tara arched up to take each one, rocking against his cock in return, over and over until her pleasure became pure need. Gripping her hip harder, he anchored himself deep inside her pussy as she thrust against him, the base of his cock hitting her clit with perfect pressure. Xander's movements grew faster, his expression so open and intense that it stole Tara's breath. Her orgasm tore through her, making her tremble and gasp. He stilled on a thrust seconds later, his entire beautiful body going bowstring tight before he exhaled with a shudder.

Time passed, although Tara had no clue how much. All she knew was Xander's body on hers, his breath growing slower even as his heart beat steady against her chest. Finally, he untangled their bodies and slipped through a door she assumed was a bathroom, gone for only a minute before he returned to her side. They didn't speak, but they didn't have to.

As Xander pulled her under the covers and tucked her in at his side, she knew there wasn't a place on the planet she would rather be.

10

Xander had never had a picture-perfect life. But with Tara lying next to him, warm and curled in at his side, he couldn't think of a better word to describe the feeling that was coursing through him.

It wasn't just that she was perfect, although, damn, she really was. But with her, *he* felt perfect, too. Like his past didn't make him. Like all of those bad things he'd seen and done had been part of getting him where he was rather than part of who he was now. Like he was worthy of this, lying here with a woman like Tara in his arms.

I want all of you, Xander. No matter what.

His heart clattered at the memory of her words. It would be easy to believe she'd said them in the heat of the moment —after all, the moment had been fucking scorching. But she'd looked at him so reverently, her fingers on his scar and her beautiful brown eyes wide open, that he knew she meant it.

All he had to do was trust her.

"You're very quiet," Tara murmured, her breath soft on

his neck. "You want to talk about whatever's going on up here?"

She reached up to glide her fingers over his temple, and the simple touch unlocked him. "There's a reason I always tell you I'm not a nice guy."

She stilled, but didn't shrink back. "Okay."

Xander knew she wasn't agreeing as much as giving him space to talk to her, and God help him, he took it. "North Point might not be all that far from here in terms of miles, but it might as well be another galaxy in other ways. You've kind of only got two choices growing up in The Hill. You either survive, or you don't. And you learn pretty quick that everyone there will do anything to survive."

"How old were you when you learned?" Tara asked.

"Seven." He didn't even have to think about it. Fuck, but he'd know this memory—one of his first—until the day he died. "My dad was never in the picture, really, and my mom worked three jobs, so she left me with Kennedy most of the time. Kennedy's only five years older than me, but she was more like a mom than a sister." All those nights she'd done her best to distract him from how cold their shitty, one-room apartment was, or used all her creativity to tape up the holes in his shoes so they could last just a little longer before she had to cave in and scratch together the money for a new-to-him pair from the thrift store three blocks over.

Xander set those memories aside in favor of the one Tara had asked for. "It was dinnertime, and I was so hungry. School was out, so we didn't have a guaranteed breakfast or lunch. That day, Kennedy and I hadn't been lucky enough to get either. We scrounged for change, but there's nothing you can do with forty cents when you're as hungry as we were. Kennedy even went next door to ask our neighbor if he could spare anything—just a couple pieces of bread and some peanut butter, a can of beans. Pizza crust, God, we'd have taken anything. But all the guy had was cheap beer."

"I'm so sorry," Tara said quietly, her tone turning the words genuine rather than oh-you-poor-charity-case-you. "No one should ever be hungry like that, let alone a child."

She wasn't wrong, and yet... "It was our normal. Kennedy knew we had to eat. She knew we were out of options." Xander took a breath, knowing he couldn't go back once he told her the rest.

But he felt steady in her arms. He trusted her. So, he said, "We walked about four miles—far enough to get out of The Hill, proper—until we got closer to a more decent part of North Point. We waited in the alley behind this bakery for what felt like forever, until the woman working there took out their trash for the night. There were probably a dozen pastries and bagels that hadn't sold mixed in with all the rest of the trash. They were as stale and soggy as hell, barely edible, really, but Kennedy and I didn't care. We dug through the trash to find them and we didn't miss a crumb. We were that fucking desperate."

"Oh, Xander. You were just trying to survive," Tara said, and the truth of it snapped under Xander's skin.

"That's just it, though. I was always just trying to survive. It starts with things like picking through the trash, or sneaking into the YMCA just to get a shower with hot water. But then you start to realize you'll do anything. You'll toss your moral compass out the fucking window. You'll lie. You'll steal. You'll hate the people who have more than you. And I did *all* of those things."

The words poured out of him now, unstoppable. "When you grow up like I did, when you are who I am, the lines start out blurry and they only get worse as you go. Good and bad are all second to surviving, and pretty soon, you just forget that there's a right and wrong. All you know is trying to get through another day, no matter what you have to do to make that happen. I did"—he broke off, his heart pounding so hard he was sure it would break free from his rib cage —"fuck, Tara, I did terrible things. I pushed Kennedy away when she found a way out of The Hill. I let a madman convince me that revenge would make me happy, and I lied and stole and worked the system to try and get it. I let myself believe that the bad things I did were justified, that it was all just the way things worked when you lived like I did. Other people were hurt—*badly*—by what I did, and I'm never going to be able to erase that."

Pulling back, Tara turned to her side, her eyes bright on his even in the shadows of his bedroom. "No, you're not," she said, and her honesty hit him with an odd sense of relief. "But that doesn't make you a bad person."

"I'm not so sure about that," Xander said, but Tara remained completely firm.

"I am one *hundred* percent sure of that. Look, if there's one thing I know above all others, it's that you can't change the past. But all those things you did, even the bad ones, are part of you. They got you *here*. They made you who you are, and who you are is a good man."

Christ, how he wanted that to be true. He ached for it from his breath to his bones. But, still... "It's hard for me to believe that sometimes."

"Well, then let me help you out." Reaching toward him, Tara ran her fingers over his forearm until she found his scar. "This may be part of you. But this"—her hand slid to his temple—"gave you what you needed to get back to your sister. And this"—her palm unfolded over the center of his chest, so warm and sweet and good he could fucking cry —"made you want to become a cop so you could help people. It's the part that loves your sister and brings Amour dinner and chills me out with random stories about rubber ducks. Yes, you've done bad things. But you're still a good man, Xander. You deserve good things. I will always believe that. Maybe it's time you did, too."

And right there, in the dark of his bedroom with Tara's arms around him, for the first time ever, he did.

TARA'S STOMACH let out a growl that could've roused a dead man. She folded both hands over her belly in an effort to hush the thing—*hello*, body betrayal—but Xander was a cop. Sharp. Intuitive. Trained to notice every detail.

Her cover was totally blown.

"Hungry?" Xander asked, looking up from his spot at the other end of his couch, where he'd been watching security footage on a closed-circuit loop on his laptop.

"No, I...well, maybe," she admitted, because he knew her well enough by now to know when she was bending the truth, and she knew *him* well enough to know he'd totally call her on it. "I kind of skipped lunch. But we're less than two weeks from the trial now, and we still haven't found the guy who attacked Amour."

"It *is* frustrating that we can't pin down the asshole who hurt her, and it also sucks that we can't tie Sansone to the attack yet," Xander agreed. "But they're both lying low. That's not entirely bad. The longer they're quiet, the safer Amour is."

"Unless Sansone is just biding his time, looking for a way to hurt her," Tara said, worry twisting in her chest.

"He's not going to find one," Xander said. "Amour is as safe as we can possibly make her." He lifted his laptop as proof. "We're monitoring the building with video and in-person surveillance. She's got a panic button with her at all times, and a tracking monitor that will make an unholy racket if she gets more than four feet from the threshold of the apartment. Capelli's keeping tabs on her cell, her email, even her place in North Point. If anyone tries to hurt her, they're going to get caught before they even get close."

Tara blew out a breath. "I know. You're absolutely right. I just can't help but feel like there isn't so much as another shoe that's going to drop as a two-ton boulder."

"No boulders," Xander said, putting his laptop aside and leaning in to kiss her. "Anyway, you've been working even harder than we have over in Intelligence. There's no way Sansone isn't going down for murder, and we're still working the case as hard as ever on our side. We'll find the guy who hurt her."

Tara looked at the various legal pads and files scattered over the coffee table by her own laptop, and okay, he wasn't wrong about her channeling pretty much all of her waking time into this case over the past week. "I hope you're right."

Her stomach chose that moment to sound off again, and Xander stood, reaching for her hands. "Okay, that's it. Come on."

"Where are we going?" she asked, although she placed her hands in his and let him pull her to her feet without pause.

"You've been working non-stop. Yes, it's for the best reason," he added, as if he'd anticipated she'd argue (which, okay, she'd planned to). "But you still need to take a break and eat, and I just so happen to know a great place nearby."

Returning her stare to the pile of work on the coffee table, Tara hesitated. But her temples throbbed and her eyes burned from alternating between the glare of her laptop and the Mount Everest of notes she'd taken. Plus, Xander was right. She *did* have to eat eventually, no matter how badly she wanted to catch a break in this case.

"Sounds great."

They made their way from his apartment to the street, which was finally cool enough to make the two-block walk to his car comfortable. Tara's nerves unwound with each passing second they walked hand in hand, although her mind still swam with thoughts of the trial. The short trip into downtown Remington had barely registered before it was behind them, and Xander pulled up in front of a brightly lit bar and grille.

"You ready for the best onion rings of your life, fresh out of the fryer?" he asked, and Tara's gut panged behind her jeans. God, had she really been distracted enough by this case not to realize he'd take her to his sister's restaurant?

"Are you sure about this?" she asked, eyeing the bustling dining room through the large front windows. "I mean, your sister and her husband and, like, everybody is all in there, right?"

"Probably." He nodded. "The crew at Station Seventeen isn't on shift tonight, and it *is* Friday. Everyone from the Thirty-Third is bound to be here, too. One big, happy family."

The thought should overwhelm her, she knew. Such a big, tightly knit group of friends, all of them caring for each other—honestly, it should scare the hell out of her. Yet somehow, with Xander sitting right there beside her, it didn't.

Nothing did.

But this was Xander, guarded and tough, so she said, "Yeah, but they're *your* big, happy family. I know you like to keep your personal stuff close to the vest, so if you think—"

"I think," he said, pulling her close for a kiss that hushed her words in the best possible way, "that you are my personal stuff. Unless the thought of meeting everybody makes you uncomfortable."

His eyes flickered with concern, but Tara shook her head. "No. I'd actually really like that."

"Good. Me, too."

They got out of the car and headed through the front door. The wait for familiar faces was short, a chorus of voices bursting up from a table by the front window.

"Hey!" Isabella stood, her eyes twinkling in welcome as she tugged first Xander, then Tara, into a pair of hugs. "We were hoping you two would show up tonight."

"Oh." Tara blinked. "Well, we were working on the case, but decided to take a break."

Isabella squeezed Tara's arm. "I'm glad. Everyone needs a breather. While we're in here, there is no case."

"Damn, babe. You've come a long way," came a male voice from beside Isabella, and she rolled her eyes playfully even though she put a healthy swat to the guy's not-small biceps.

"Mmm. Tara, have you met my smartass husband?" Isabella asked, and the dark-haired guy flashed Tara a killer smile.

"Kellan Walker. It's nice to finally meet you."

"You, too," Tara said, her smile in return practically involuntary at his kind welcome.

"These guys have said great things about you." Kellan extended one hand in greeting as he used the other to thumb a gesture toward the group at the table behind him, where Garza and Hollister sat with Capelli and a woman with a light brown ponytail and a curious-as-hell stare.

"They're all true," Xander put in, and Kellan turned toward him with a laugh.

"I don't doubt it. But I was *not* saying nice things about you the other night when you were kicking my ass up and down the basketball court. You dick."

The handshake/half-embrace/back-slap that followed took all the heat out of the words, and Xander answered just as easily. "You know I'm going to do it again next week, don't you?"

"We'll see, hotshot. We'll see."

"Oh, my God, stop drowning this poor woman in testosterone," the other woman at the table said, shaking her head apologetically at Tara. "We can't take them anywhere, really. Shae McCullough." She stood and extended her hand warmly. "It really is great to meet you, all chest thumping aside."

"Oh, you're the adrenaline junkie," Tara blurted, clamping down on her lip a millisecond too late.

But everyone at the table just laughed, Shae the loudest. "I see the rookie's been doing me justice. I knew I liked you," she said, ruffling Xander's hair.

"Hey, it's not my fault you live to rappel down six-story buildings and elevator shafts," Xander pointed out, returning Shae's hello hug with a grin.

"You really did do her justice. She'll jump off of nearly anything as long as her gear will hold," Capelli said, a rare smile on his serious face that probably had everything to do with the way the female firefighter had just leaned in to kiss him.

"Come on, honey. What else are buildings for if not to scale them?"

Oh, Tara *liked* her.

The group made room for her and Xander to sit down,

and a passing server took their order for a much-needed dinner. The conversation flowed back and forth with ease, sometimes between the entire group, and other times among smaller side discussions. Quinn and Luke Slater wandered over from the group of firefighters hanging out in the alcove by the pool table to say hello and ask how Amour was doing, both of them seeming genuinely glad to hear of her full recovery. The pair said their goodbyes not long after, though, and Tara sat back to soak in the happy chatter around her.

"You fit right in," Garza said from the seat next to her, his voice low enough to keep the observation between them in the din of the restaurant.

"Doesn't seem too hard with this group," Tara replied. Everyone had been so nice, welcoming her into the fold with their questions and stories and jokes. She was still a little nervous to meet Kennedy, who Xander had gone to say a quick hello to but was currently working her way through the last throes of the dinner rush. Other than that, Tara had felt shockingly right at home.

"Yes and no." Garza took a draw from the beer bottle between his fingers, his dark eyes surveying the group as they chatted away. "Don't get me wrong. They're good team-mates. The best I've ever had, actually."

His pause lasted for a beat, but Tara waited it out patiently. This was definitely a side of the detective she'd never seen before—he was usually over and out in under seven syllables. She didn't mind giving him space, though, and after another moment, he took it.

"I guess it just depends on what baggage you bring to the table, you know? They're quick to accept the people who have their backs, but..."

"Sometimes it's hard to let them?" Tara supplied,

laughing softly when Garza's dark brows lifted in surprise. "Yeah, I actually know a thing or two about that, as it turns out. But I'm slowly learning that it's worth it to trust the right people."

One corner of Garza's mouth kicked up into what Tara would bet was as close as he got to a smile. "Right people, or right *person*?"

His gaze shot meaningfully to Xander, who was absorbed in conversation with Kellan and Isabella, and even though Tara's cheeks heated, she didn't shy away from the question.

"The right person can change everything." At Garza's look of doubt, she added, "You don't think so?"

"No shade intended," he said quietly, lifting his hands. "For you, it's clearly true, and that's cool. You and the rookie deserve to be happy."

"But not you," she said.

If Garza minded her forthright question, he didn't show it. "For me, happy's a little more complicated. I'm more of a 'casual person' kind of guy."

Well, that was hardly shocking. Objectively speaking, Garza was good-looking as hell, with that dark and broody thing going on that made most women want to fling their panties around. He probably had no shortage of people wanting to share his bed, even short-term.

"I don't think I ever would've believed the whole 'one right person' thing before now. I'm still trying to get my head around it, to be honest," Tara admitted.

"You look like you're knocking it out of the park," Garza said, taking a long draw from his beer. "Maybe you should just run with it."

Tara looked at Xander, his expression laid back and his

smile growing wide as he met her gaze from across the table and held on tight.

Yeah. It was too late to run with it. Her heart had already taken a huge head start, and being with Xander felt far too good not to let the rest of her follow.

11

Xander sat back in his seat at the Intelligence
Unit's usual table and felt like one lucky son of a
bitch. He'd known bringing Tara here was a
gamble—the guarded way she'd always listened to him talk
about his big, loud found family spoke volumes about her
hesitation to let anyone get too close. But she'd seemed so in
need of support, of people who'd care that she'd had a shit
week and do their level best to lift her spirits, and, God,
Xander didn't know any better group for the job.

These people always had his back. And he wanted to
always have Tara's back. Bringing her here had just felt right.

There was just one thing left to do.

"I'm going to head to the bar and grab a drink," he said
to Tara, gesturing to the back of the restaurant. "Do you
want to come with me and see if Kennedy can take a break?"

God love her, she didn't hesitate. "Sure."

Tara said a quick goodbye to Garza, who she'd been
quietly chatting up for a little while as Xander had hung out
with the rest of the group. Reaching down low for her hand,
Xander headed for the bar. His heart thumped out a

reminder of Kennedy's reservations about Tara, and even though the charges against him were ancient history now, he knew better than to mess with fate.

"So, um, my sister can be a little...protective," he said, selecting his words with care.

Tara laughed. "She practically raised you, Xander. That's hardly shocking."

"Right. It's just that Kennedy can kind of take it to a whole new level from time to time, and you and I didn't exactly have the smoothest start two years ago."

"Ah." Tara stopped, turning toward him. "So, she's worried I might hurt you."

Shit. "To be fair, she worries about a lot when it comes to me. But, yeah. That's probably accurate."

"It's totally okay if she's tough on me," Tara said, and wait...

"What?"

Tara's smile was so wide-open and beautiful, Xander nearly lost his fucking breath. "First of all, I face people who are tough on me every time I go to court. It's literally what I do for a living. But, more importantly, if Kennedy needs me to earn her trust, I'm okay with that. She's wary because she loves you, and I'm more than happy to show her I care about you, too."

For a heartbeat, Xander was stuck in place, trying like hell to name the feeling flying through his chest. But Tara was right here in front of him, and suddenly that was all that mattered.

"Okay," he said, pulling her close and kissing her even though they were in the middle of a crowded bar full of his family and friends. "Then let's go."

They finished the trip to the bar in less than a dozen steps, heading toward the spot at the bend in the L-shaped bar, where Gamble always—yep, there he was, the big bruiser—parked himself whenever he was in the house. Kennedy was on the business end of the bar, popping the caps off a pair of beers for a couple of the guys on Station Seventeen's Rescue Squad, and she met his gaze with a smile as he approached.

"I was beginning to think you'd forgotten your way back here," she said, because, of course, it was her birthright to give him shit whenever possible. "Although I guess now that you're part of the Intelligence crew, hanging at their table is going to be your new normal."

"It's one case, Ken," Xander murmured, even though he couldn't help but like the idea of being part of the Intelligence Unit one day. "And we're not talking about it, remember?"

She lifted her hands in apology. "Nope. It seems we have other things to talk about."

Her eyes landed on Tara, and yeah, that was his cue to just rip off the Band-Aid. "Kennedy, this is Tara Kingston. Tara, meet my sister, Kennedy, and her husband, Ian."

Gamble was closer, so he extended a hand first. "Gamble," he said. "No one really calls me Ian unless they're serving me with a summons or something."

"You're safe with me on that end, for sure," Tara said with a smile. Turning toward Kennedy, she said, "It's really nice to officially meet you. I've been enjoying carry-out from this place for weeks now, and I have to say, the food is every bit as good as Xander brags."

Kennedy's dark brows winged up, but only for a second before her expression softened at the words. "We do our best. It's good to see you under better circumstances than last time."

Xander's pulse sped up at the reference to the case two

years ago, but Tara didn't blink. "I'm dedicated to my job, just like I know you're dedicated to your brother. I'm really glad it all worked out for the best. The RPD is certainly the better for it with Xander in their ranks."

"That's the truth," Gamble said, eyeing Kennedy, who—thank fuck—nodded.

"I'm still not wild about you potentially being in harm's way, but if I can be married to a guy who runs into burning buildings"—she cracked what Xander would bet was an involuntary smile as she looked over the bar at Gamble—"I guess I can figure out how to deal with it."

"So, how did you two meet, anyway?" Tara asked, and Kennedy's smile became a full-on laugh.

"Would you believe he hauled me out of here when the bar was on fire?"

"Not to put too fine a point on it, but I met this guy while trying to prosecute him," Tara said, tilting her head in Xander's direction. "So, yep. I would absolutely believe that's how you met."

Tara took a seat at the bar with Xander beside her on one side and Gamble on the other as Kennedy launched into the story. He knew it by heart, of course—for Chrissake, he'd been there, at least for the PG-13 parts of it. But listening to his sister tell the story, with Gamble popping in a few well-placed flourishes and reminders ("I'd like the record to show that I made it out of that building without a scratch. Not *one*, and she was still mad.") made Xander realize once again how perfectly suited for each other they were. With each genuine question Tara asked and each moment she listened, Kennedy softened further. The conversation swung around to Tara and Xander, and even though they couldn't really talk about the case they were working, they still had plenty to say ("did you know he calmed me down with a story about 28,000 rubber ducks?" Tara had asked, only to have Kennedy laugh and reply, "That sounds like something he'd do."). Sitting there with Tara beside him felt like the most natural thing in the world, to the point that Xander would've laughed at the reminder that he'd been so wary of being with her in the first place.

It felt right. *She* felt right, beside him.

Finally, after her beer was long gone and the laughter dwindled down, Tara said, "Okay, if I don't excuse myself to the ladies room, I may float away."

"It's down the hall, to the left," Gamble said, pointing. "Actually, I need to ask McCullough a question before she and Capelli get out of here for the night, and she's over by the pool table. It's on the way, so I can walk you."

"Perfect," Tara said. Sliding to her feet, she turned to follow Gamble, swinging back at the last second to press a kiss over Xander's cheek and murmur, "Be back in a minute," before following Gamble into the thinning crowd.

"I never thought I'd say this," Kennedy said as soon as Tara was out of earshot, and God, it should've been warning enough. "But a) I really like her, and b) you are fucking smitten."

"I'm not *smitten*," Xander argued, although his laugh kind of killed the seriousness he'd wanted to stick to the delivery.

Kennedy, being Kennedy, snorted. "Oh, look. You're smitten *and* full of shit. Also, crazy about that woman."

Aw, hell. He couldn't exactly deny what his sister had said. But still... "Do you really think a woman like her and a guy like me can make something work in the long run?"

Pressing her forearms over the bar, Kennedy leaned toward him, so close that he had no choice but to meet her stare or be called out for dodging her. "What I think is that it's far past time for you to realize you're not the same man you were two years ago."

"It's not that easy," Xander said, but Kennedy wasn't having it.

"It *is* that easy. Xander, everybody fucks up, and people like me and you? We have walls. They're there for a reason," she added, because she had to know he'd say so. They never would have survived without them. "But it's okay to let people past them."

"You say that like it's easy," Xander said, his voice low.

Kennedy's laugh in reply, however? Rang halfway across the bar. "And you say that like I don't know it. You think that story of how Gamble and I met was all hearts and flowers?"

And now Xander wanted to laugh. "You're hardly the type. Either of you."

"And you think I didn't fight it like a heavyweight once I realized I was breaking all my cardinal rules of survival by actually falling for him?"

Xander was her *brother*. Of course they'd never really talked about her and Gamble like that. But that still couldn't stop him from saying, "No. But—"

"No 'buts'," Kennedy said, her voice going soft over the words as she reached out to squeeze his arm. "You can still be beautiful even if you're a little broken, and the look on Tara's face says she wants you, exactly as you are. Falling for someone is scary—trust me, I know. But that doesn't mean you shouldn't do it, Xander."

Of course, she was too late, because Xander knew that despite his defenses and his past and all the darkness that went with it, he'd already fallen truly, wildly in love with Tara.

∾

Tara had never realized that sheer, bone-breaking exhaustion could be coupled with so much bliss. The exhaustion came from having worked twelve to fourteen hour days over the last week and a half, prepping Amour and the Intelligence detectives for their testimony and making sure every single case detail was exactly as it should be, locked and loaded and ready to nail Ricky Sansone to the wall.

The bliss, she blamed on Xander. Not that she was mad about it. In fact, between the days they'd spent working on the case and the nights they'd spent tangled in both amazing conversation and each other's arms (not to mention a few other, more provocative body parts), Tara was actually the opposite of mad about it.

And the whole thing felt too right, too purely, perfectly good, for that to scare her.

"Hey," came a voice from beside her, and speak of the sweet and sexy devil. "Am I late?"

"Nope. You're right on time," Tara said, her smile involuntary and huge. She fought the urge to kiss him—not that she didn't want to, because Xander + that uniform = so, *so* hot. But since they were standing less than ten feet away from the Intelligence Unit's main office, and the doors leading in to said space were made of glass (bulletproof, naturally, but super-duper see-through all the same), she figured she should at least try to remain professional and hope that she still had a tiny bit of game in the poker face department.

One corner of Xander's mouth kicked up into a smile, and yep, so much for that. "How was the meeting with Judge Waters today?" he asked, pulling the door open for her and following her lead into the open space.

"Interesting. I'll fill everyone in as soon as we get started," Tara said. Thankfully, Isabella, Capelli, Garza, and Sinclair were already waiting. This was definitely something they were all going to want to hear.

"Well, if it isn't my favorite dynamic duo." Isabella shot them a grin from behind her desk, making Capelli tilt his head in thought.

"That's quite a clever play on words, actually. Linking Xander and Tara together now that they're a couple."

Garza shook his head as Xander flushed and Tara studied the case board with laser-like focus. "Subtle, dude. So very subtle."

"What?" Capelli asked. "Are we not supposed to know they're a couple? I mean, they're not making it all that hard to figure out. Plus, there aren't any rules against it, in this case. Article Nine, Section One Twenty-Seven of the city of Remington's Code of Ethics and Business Conduct specifically states—"

"Capelli," Sinclair interrupted smoothly, saving Tara and Xander from the hot seat. "Maybe we could stick to a more relevant topic of conversation? Just for now?"

"Oh. Right." Capelli dipped his head in apology. "Sorry, my brain just...anyway. Let me patch Amour in through the secure line."

"Great. Thank you," Sinclair said. Seconds later, Amour's face popped up on one of the digital screens. "Hi, Amour. This is Sergeant Sinclair. How are you doing over there?"

"Okay, I guess," she said. With her hair pulled back and her face washed clean of makeup, she looked even younger than her eighteen years, and Tara wanted nothing more than to crawl through the screen and hug the poor girl. "I kind of just want this over with. No offense."

"None taken, kid," Garza said, sending his stare in Tara's direction. "What've we got from the judge?"

Tara's thoughts fell back to a few hours ago. "Sansone's lawyer argued against Amour testifying via closed circuit with her identity hidden. He said there's no credible threat against her, his client would never hurt anyone, pulled out all the theatrics." She paused to roll her eyes. "I argued that due to the nature of the charges and the testimony she was going to deliver, not to mention the attack and its accompanying threat, there was every reason for her to fear for her life. Judge Waters agreed that even though there's no evidence that Sansone was behind the attack, our fears are reasonable. Sansone didn't like it one bit, though."

"How do you know?" Sinclair asked, and Tara suppressed a shiver.

"I saw the two of them talking in the hallway at the courthouse after the meeting. Sansone must've been waiting."

Isabella's brows popped. "*That's* interesting."

"It's telling," Garza countered. "He must be pretty worried to show up in person."

"Well, he looked furious. He even gave me a menacing look on my way out," Tara said. Dirty looks were far from abnormal in her line of work, and her creep-o-meter had a pretty high threshold, but Sansone? Ugh, he unnerved her.

Xander's shoulders tensed beneath his crisp blue uniform shirt. "Did he say anything to you?" he asked, and wait, why were Capelli *and* Sinclair leaning in to hear her answer?

"No." That awful, dead-eyed stare had been plenty. "Why?"

Capelli's pause lasted for less than a beat. "We've caught some suspicious activity around the safe house this week. Nothing definitive," he added, and only then did Tara notice that both she and Xander had jerked to attention. "There's no overt threat, and Amour's just fine. Right?"

"Yeah." Amour nodded on screen, looking apologetically at both Xander and Tara. "They just told me this morning, otherwise I'd have said something when you guys were here last night. But I'm okay."

The way she chewed her bottom lip said otherwise, but that was a hair Tara would have to split later. "What kind of suspicious activity are we talking about, exactly?"

Garza exchanged a look with Sinclair, then Capelli, before gesturing to the case board on the screen next to Amour's video feed. "We're tracking everyone who goes in and out of the building. Because all of the residents have key cards and all guests have to be buzzed in, it's been pretty easy to do, for the most part. And nearly everyone has a pattern of some kind."

"That makes sense," Xander said. "Work schedules, takeout on Friday nights. The gym, church, even the grocery store—people usually do all those things on a schedule."

Isabella nodded. "So, when we noticed one resident's card being used when she's normally at work, it tripped our notice. Or, more specifically, Capelli's notice."

Okay, wow. Tara knew the guy was good, but... "You noticed one deviation among hundreds of residents and thousands of comings and goings?"

"I have an eidetic memory," he said with a shrug. "I notice everything. If I'm being honest, it's not as great as you might think. But in this case, it proved useful, because Yolanda Martinez's key card was being used by someone who is definitely not her."

A grainy image appeared on the case board screen. "Yolanda's card was used to access the building three times two days ago, and none of them were by her. The first was at ten thirty AM, the second at eleven forty-two, and the third at one fifteen."

The screen shot of a man built like a linebacker-lumberjack hybrid made Tara's heart pound. His hoodie, coupled with a baseball cap pulled low over his face, made it impossible to get a good look at any identifying features, but it was easy to see that the guy was just plain huge.

Also, *not* Yolanda. "Let me guess. Ms. Martinez doesn't know this man."

"She reported her card missing three hours after its last use," Garza confirmed.

"Does he look familiar to you?" Tara asked Amour hopefully.

She shook her head. "No. I mean, he looks like the right size, but I never saw his face in the first place. I only heard his voice. I'm sorry."

"It's okay," Xander said quickly. "We're still going to keep you safe."

At that, Sinclair nodded. "We've got a heightened alert on the building surveillance. Hale and Maxwell are there now. Our guy is smart enough to know where the building's security cameras are."

"He avoided them whenever he could," Garza added, and Capelli brought up a quick loop of footage on the screen. "But he couldn't dodge the one in the elevator. He never looks up, but every time, he gets off on the fourth floor, stays for about ten minutes, then leaves."

Confusion sent Tara's brows downward. "Okay, but Amour is on the fifth floor."

"There are no cameras in the stairwells," Xander said, realization in his voice. "He could've easily walked up a flight, just to throw off anyone watching."

Isabella sent him a look that read *I'm impressed*. "That's our theory, too. It's all just a little too suspicious to be someone casing the building for robberies."

"So, what's the plan, then? We still have a couple weeks before the trial," Tara said. "We have to make sure Amour stays safe."

"We'll keep doing what we're doing," Sinclair said, gesturing to the case board. "Hollister teamed up with Dade for a canvas of the building on the off chance that someone remembers seeing this guy. Once residents find out there was a suspicious person in the building, they'll lean toward being hypervigilant, which also works in our favor."

"Sansone is starting to get desperate, just like we wanted him to," Isabella said, splitting her gaze between Tara and Amour. "And while I know that sounds frightening, it's actually a good thing. Desperate means impulsive, and impulsive means sloppy."

"It's still not without risk." Reaching into one of his desk drawers, Capelli pulled out a necklace, then looked at Tara. "We'd like you to wear this tracker as a precaution."

Shock rippled through her. "Me? Wouldn't it be smarter for Amour to have one?"

"She does," Capelli said. "But as we get closer to the trial, you two are going to be together quite a bit. If we can track you, we can also keep tabs on her. It's essentially a failsafe."

Oh. That did seem smart. "I suppose it wouldn't hurt. But it still seems kind of over the top."

"It's not over the top if it keeps you safe," Xander said, a strange intensity flashing through his eyes so quickly, she couldn't be certain she'd seen it, let alone name it.

"Trust me." Isabella gave up a knowing smile. "They're not so over the top. Those little babies can save your life."

Before Tara could ask for the story behind her comment —and there was *totally* a story there—Amour let out a gasp, stealing everyone's attention, along with Tara's composure.

"Oh, my God," she said, her eyes wide with fear even as they were glued to the burner phone Capelli had given her.

"What?" Xander asked, his body on full alert, muscles coiled tight. "What's the matter?"

"This."

She turned the phone toward the camera, and Tara's blood froze in her veins.

I KNOW WHERE YOU'RE HIDING.

12

T ara triple-checked every last square inch of Amour's apartment before she allowed herself to exhale.

"Okay. Everything looks clear."

Amour raised a brow at Tara from the spot where she stood in the bedroom doorway. "You know you're, like, the fourth person to check, right?"

At that, Tara had to eke out a tiny smile. "And you know I'm a perfectionist, right? Plus, we can't be too safe."

Case in point: Maxwell and Hale had arrived at the apartment less than two minutes after the text message had appeared on Amour's phone a few hours ago to scour it from rug to rafters. In the meantime, Capelli had run the ominous text message through every program he had. The message had been delivered to the burner via a source that had—so far—bounced off no less than a dozen cell towers from Norway to North Carolina. Identical texts had gone to several hundred cell phones, all of which had been within a mile of Amour's location at the time.

The message had likely been a scare tactic aimed at a lucky guess, but Tara couldn't deny the truth.

It had fucking worked.

"Are you sure you don't want me to stay with you tonight in the new safe house?" Tara asked, also for the fourth time. "I really don't mind."

Amour shook her head. "Detective Hale is already crashing with me tonight. Plus, I'm sure Xander would miss you."

Tara's shock must've been Sharpied all over her face, because Amour smirked. "Oh, my God, you guys are so obvious. Of course I know you're all into each other, or whatever."

"I am pretty into him. Or whatever," Tara admitted. Her soft laugh seemed to break the tension, and she stepped toward Amour. "And we'll both still only be one phone call away if you need anything at all. Even if it's late at night. Okay?"

"Yeah." Pulling the sleeve of her sweatshirt over one hand, she fidgeted with the fraying cuff. "So, are we still going to do the practice thing tomorrow for the trial?"

Tara proceeded with extreme caution. Nearly all key witnesses felt jittery as a trial date loomed closer, and she'd had to talk far more than a few off the ledge of indecision. "If you feel like you're up for it."

"Sansone knows it's me, right? I mean, there's no way he doesn't know."

Shit. "It certainly seems so. We don't have reports of anyone else from the club being threatened, and he's got to know the person testifying has insider information that only an employee would have."

"So if he knows it's me, what's stopping me from testifying in person? You know, like, in the courtroom with him."

Tara blinked, thoroughly stunned. "It's still risky. There's a chance he could be bluffing. It's probably a small chance," she added. "But we have to take every precaution to keep you safe."

"Okay, but won't it make what I have to say more compelling if I'm there in person and the jury can see me?"

"Compelling?" Tara echoed, and wait a second... "Where did you come up with that idea?"

Amour flushed, her gaze landing on the floor. "I've been stuck in this apartment for weeks. Did you really think I wouldn't surf the Internet? Anyway, it's true, right? In-person testimony is more impactful when a jury can see the witness."

"In most cases, that's true," Tara admitted slowly. She wasn't about to lie to the girl. "But there have been plenty of cases where a witness was very compelling even when their identity was masked."

"Do you think it would be better for the case if I was there?"

"I would never ask you to take that risk."

"You're totally not answering the question," Amour pointed out, and God, she was a lot tougher than Tara had given her credit for.

"I think that I have enough time to prep you for taking the stand in person and making it very, very difficult for Sansone to be acquitted," she said with care. "But you have to understand, it's still very dangerous."

"I do understand, and I don't want him to hurt me. But I also don't want him to get away with what he did. Watching you and seeing how hard you're working on this case... you're showing me not to give up. You'll do whatever it takes to put him away. I want to do whatever it takes, too. I don't want to be scared anymore."

Tara reached out and squeezed Amour's arms gently, her heart beating fast, but full of hope. "I'll talk to my boss and Sergeant Sinclair. *If* they agree that we can outweigh the risks, we'll talk about it. Fair enough?"

"Fair enough."

And just when Tara didn't think she could be any more surprised by the conversation, Amour reached out to fold her arms around Tara.

"Thanks for always having my back."

"Of course," Tara said, hugging her tight. "I'll be right here with you, all the way to the end. I'll keep you safe, no matter what."

"Are you absolutely sure you don't want to go over the plan just one more time?"

Okay, so Tara knew she was bordering on overkill, and the wry look on Xander's face confirmed it. But in mere hours, she'd call Amour to the stand, placing her face to face with Sansone and erasing any doubt of her identity from his evil little mind. Yes, Tara's boss and Sinclair had taken every precaution imaginable to keep the younger woman safe—including a security detail that rivaled those of most pop stars—and more yes, Sansone had been church-mouse quiet ever since Amour had received that text threat, leading Capelli to believe that the message had been more of a lucky guess than a true concern. To top it off, Amour had been unshakably strong even during the most grueling parts of the preparations, when Tara had cross-examined her so meanly, most other people would've crumbled like a sandcastle on a sunny day.

And still, Tara couldn't shake the instinct in the pit of

her belly that said Sansone was just biding his time. Waiting to strike. Waiting to hurt Amour again.

Please, please, just keep her and Xander safe.

Xander crossed the kitchen, putting down his coffee mug before cupping her face to kiss her, bringing her back to reality. "You know what? Going over the plan one more time probably won't hurt," he said. She knew he was humoring her, and God, she loved him for it.

Blinking past the shock of the thought—where the hell had *that* come from?—she cleared her throat and focused on his voice, calm and steady as he said, "Okay. Here's the plan. I'm going to leave in five minutes to meet Garza and Sinclair. We're picking Amour up at the safe house at seven AM."

Tara nodded. Hearing the plan out loud, even though she knew it by heart, smoothed out her nerves, allowing her to breathe deeply as he continued.

"We'll take her to the courthouse, where she'll have a private waiting room. You'll meet us there at eight thirty to make sure everything is set—which it will be, because Isabella and Capelli will make sure of it, down to the very smallest security detail. Then, Judge Waters will start promptly at nine, and you and Amour will stick it to Sansone so thoroughly, he'll never breathe free air again. Did I miss anything?"

"Only the part where you're fantastic," Tara said, pressing up to kiss him.

Xander smiled against her mouth. "You're pretty fantastic, too. But if I don't head out, I'm going to be *late* and fantastic."

"Not today." She pulled back and pointed at the door with mock seriousness. "Go. Just promise me you'll be careful."

"I will," he said, kissing her one last time before heading for the door. Even though she had a little time before she had to get dressed and head to the courthouse, she had far too much nervous energy to sit around Xander's apartment. After a quick shower, Tara put on her lucky suit, pulling her hair into a twist and slipping into her favorite black heels.

"You've got this," she told her reflection. "After today, this will all be history."

She didn't see the man behind her until it was too late to scream.

TARA WOKE up with the knowledge of three things. The first was that something odd must have happened to her head, because she couldn't get her thoughts to line up properly. The second was that her arms were equally affected, heavy and useless at her sides. The third was that she had no idea where she was, but it wasn't anywhere familiar, and wait... wasn't she supposed to be—

She sat up in a rush. Or, at least, she tried to. But between the screaming pain reverberating against her skull and the zip ties around both her wrists and her ankles, she didn't get very far.

"Oh, good. You're awake. As you know, I'm on a schedule, and I don't have a whole lot of time."

Tara squinted through the dingy space—a basement, maybe? No, a warehouse of some kind—her glassy gaze landing on Ricky Sansone.

Oh, God. Oh, God, oh, God. "Where's Amour?" she croaked, and Sansone's expression hardened.

"I'd guess that traitorous whore is probably at the court-house with your little boyfriend and those other fucking cops. But don't you worry, they'll all get theirs soon enough. After they have the pleasure of having to piece together your body, of course. You'll be amazed at how long it's going to take them to find all of you."

Tara's stomach roiled with the burning urge to vomit. "You have to know you're not going to get away with this."

"Please," he snorted, his footsteps echoing through the space as he circled around her, his suit pristine. "I'm absolutely going to get away with this, just like I'll get away with killing that bitch and everyone else involved in this case. You see, Blaze, here, is going to wait until I'm all settled in, nice and cozy at the courthouse before he starts to torture you."

He gestured to a huge man in the shadows, who stepped into the light just enough for Tara to see the tattoo of a Grim Reaper on his forearm, complete with tally marks on an elaborate book underneath, by his wrist.

Fresh fear spiked in her chest. "They're going to miss me in court. They'll know something's wrong."

Sansone rolled his eyes as if she were a petulant child. "Of course they will. You not being there is the entire point, you stupid twat. We can't exactly have a trial if the prosecuting attorney's a no-show, now can we?"

Realization slammed into Tara, making her temples throb and her skin ice over. "You made it look like you were going after Amour so you could come after me instead."

"Jesus, it's about time you figured it out. I was starting to think that fancy fucking degree was wasted on you. See, I've known where Amour was for a while now. The trouble is, she was too well guarded for me to do anything about it without getting caught. But I knew she'd have to come out of her hidey-hole to testify, and when she did, you'd be ripe for the picking. For fuck's sake, it took Blaze less than ten seconds to get past that lock. And everyone's so worried about that filthy slut that no one will notice you're missing until it's too late. Blaze is going to gut you like the pig you are. He'll go after Amour next, then that pregnant cop. That'll be a two-for-one."

The excitement in his smile made Tara revisit the urge to be sick, and she bit the inside of her cheek as hard as she could in order to keep hold of her quickly waning calm. "We won't miss a single person who worked this case, and I promise, every last one of you will beg for death before we finally decide to deliver it. We'll save Xander for last, though, so he doesn't miss a single second of watching the rest of you get murdered."

"Please. You can't do this," Tara said, the zip ties biting into her skin as her adrenaline made her struggle in vain. Oh, God, she had to calm down. She had to think. To *breathe.*

Interesting story. Like, thirty years ago, there was this cargo ship on its way from Hong Kong to the United States...

She was going to get out of this. Xander would find her. He *would*. He'd find her and they'd keep each other safe and they'd put Sansone away, this time for good. All she had to do was breathe.

"You're hardly in a position to tell me what I can and can't do," Sansone hissed, backhanding her expertly before glaring down into her face. "I'll be in a public courtroom when you finally bleed out, and those cops will all be dead before they can even think of tracing your murder, or any other, back to me. Have a nice life, Ms. Kingston."

He made it all the way to the door before sending a chilling look over his shoulder at her.

"What's left of it, anyway."

13

"Something's wrong."

Amour stopped, mid-pace, on her nine thousandth loop across the floor. She was wearing a nice navy blue dress with a cream-colored sweater over it, but the look on her face canceled out all of the carefully chosen clothing and practiced calm.

Xander forced his composure into submission. "It's only eight twenty," he said, looking at Garza for a reassuring nod before adding on, "she still has ten minutes, and there's plenty of time before the trial starts."

"No, something's wrong," Amour insisted. "Tara promised she'd be here. She's always early. It's, like, her thing."

Xander opened his mouth to protest...but couldn't. Damn it, she was right. Tara's version of on time was always fifteen minutes early. Which meant, right now, she was five minutes late.

And she was never late.

Flipping his cell phone into his palm, he forced his fingers not to shake as he found Tara's number and hit *send*.

"Hi, you've reached the voicemail of Tara Kingston, assistant district attorney. I'm not available to take your call right now, but..."

Something was wrong.

"It went right to voicemail," Xander said, his pulse starting to yammer at him in earnest now. "Capelli, can you ping her?"

"Sure thing," came Capelli's voice through the wireless coms he'd given to both Xander and Garza an hour ago. "Wait, this is weird. Tara's cell is still in your apartment."

"But that's impossible," Garza said, shaking his head. "She's supposed to be here in less than ten minutes, and she'd never forget..."

All at once, the truth hit Xander with breath-stealing clarity. The look Sansone had given Tara outside the judge's chambers a few weeks ago. The fact that she was just as integral to the trial as Amour.

The way he'd left her, alone and completely vulnerable in his apartment this morning, and oh, God.

"Where's Sansone? Right now, where is he?" Xander demanded.

Capelli, who was set up in a state-of-the-art mobile surveillance unit around the corner, didn't waste any time answering. "Looks like he's in a hired car, headed for the courthouse. ETA ten minutes. You don't think he—"

"I do," Xander said. How could he have been so fucking *stupid*? He lasered a stare at Garza. "I don't know how or where, but we need to find her. Right goddamn now."

"Oh, my God, this is totally my fault." Amour's eye filled with tears. Her hand flew up to fiddle with her necklace, and wait...wait!

"The tracker!" Xander bit out. "She was wearing it this morning when I left. Where is it now?"

"Oh, holy shit. It's in North Point," Capelli breathed.

Xander swung toward the door, his feet already in motion, but Garza beat him to it.

"You're going to need backup, my man, not to mention a ride. Now, let's get Amour safe with Maxwell and Hale, and go see about catching a bad guy, huh?"

Xander nodded. Now all he had to do was pray he wasn't too late.

XANDER WOULD GIVE GARZA THIS—THE guy drove like a fearless motherfucker. Not that he'd been happy about being relegated to the passenger seat, or that he'd kept quiet about his displeasure. But the ride, as swift as it'd been, had given Xander a full opportunity to cement both his wits and his will.

He was going in there for Tara, no matter what.

And no matter what, she was coming out alive.

"This is it," Xander said, spotting the unmarked car where Sinclair and Hollister had just rolled up in. The four men got out, each one undergoing a weapons check that was probably as instinctive as breathing.

"Okay, what've we got?" Sinclair asked, and damn, Hollister hadn't wasted a single drop of time.

He gestured to the thermal imaging camera he was sweeping over the warehouse, which looked abandoned, at least from the outside. "Looks like two people on the ground floor, Bravo side. One considerably larger than the other. Second person appears to be on the ground, possibly bound. Not moving."

Xander took a step toward the house, his heart fully engaged with his windpipe.

"Easy, Matthews. She's got a heat signature, which means she's okay for now," Sinclair said. "That could change on a dime if we fuck this up, so let's just take a second and think this through."

Xander wanted to scream. He wanted to get directly in Sinclair's face and tell him to get the fuck out of his path or get knocked over.

But he couldn't, because God damn it, the guy was right.

Still, Xander wasn't about to take any of this lightly. "Fine. But whatever we're going to do, let's figure it out right now, because I love that woman, and every second she's in danger is one second closer to me doing whatever it takes to get her out of there no matter *what* I have to risk."

"Well then," Garza said, the edge of his mouth hooking up into a smile. "Guess we'd better let the rookie kick in some doors in the name of romance. Here's what I'm thinking."

TARA KNEW her time was up. Blaze had dragged a table to the center of the room and proceeded to pull out a padded canvas roll like chefs used to carry their knives. Only, the tools in this case looked a crap-load more sinister, with blades and hooks and—Tara bit back a whimper—two circular saws, along with a full set of scrubs and elbow-length rubber gloves.

The only thought that soothed her in the slightest was that maybe, just maybe, she'd see Lucas soon.

But, oh, God, she was so frightened.

She started to tremble so hard that her teeth chattered. She had to keep it together, she *had* to think. Desperate, she reached into her memory, letting Xander's soothing voice wash over her.

On the route, the ship accidentally lost a shipping crate, like, smack in the middle of the Pacific Ocean. I bet you can't guess what was in it...

"Time's up." It was the first thing Blaze had said to her, and the finality of it sent panic into Tara's throat.

Twenty-eight thousand rubber ducks.

She managed to breathe. "Please," she whispered, partly to buy time and partly because she had no problem begging for her life. "Please don't do this."

"They all say that, you know. But that's fine." He walked over to her, lifting her up by one bound arm like she was nothing more than a rag doll. "You'll bleed more if you struggle."

"Freeze! Remington PD! Show me your hands!"

Xander's voice rang through Tara like a spoon against cut crystal, clear and true.

Blaze, however? Was very unimpressed. Wheeling Tara around, he pressed the blade of the knife he'd been holding against her slamming pulse. "She'll be dead before you can pull the trigger."

He'd angled Tara in front of him, using her as a shield. But that didn't stop Xander from training his gun on Blaze and saying, "And you'll be dead before you hit the floor. Your choice."

"No choice." Blaze laughed against her ear. "You won't risk it. I can smell it on you. How scared you are for her life."

He drew the blade over Tara's neck, enough pain searing through her to make her cry out.

"Stop!" Xander yelled, frustration crossing his always-calm features. "Okay, okay. What do you want?"

"Jesus, you weak fuck. You're making this too easy." Blaze

shook his head. Confusion flickered through Tara's brain—why would Xander have barged in just to give up so easily? "Put your gun down and kick it over to the corner. There you go, you pussy," he sneered as Xander did what he'd asked. "Now get over here so I can tie you up before I give you the privilege of watching her die."

Tara's mouth dropped open. But then, Blaze loosened his grip on her, lowering the knife just enough as Xander took a step forward, and Xander looked at her, his face perfectly calm as he said, "I will do anything to keep you safe, Tara. Anything."

What happened next was all slow motion. Xander's gaze flickered over Blaze's shoulder, his chin lifting in the barest nod. Bunching all of her muscles as tight as they'd go, Tara snapped her chin forward, using her momentum to smash the back of her head directly into the spot where she hoped and prayed Blaze's nose was.

Xander lunged for her at the same moment Garza burst from the shadows and smashed his pistol into the back of Blaze's head.

"Remington PD! Stand down!" Garza barked. But the words were sadly unnecessary, since Blaze had gone down like a bag of bricks.

And Tara was in Xander's arms. Safe. She was safe.

They were all safe.

"Shit, babe. You're bleeding," he said, reaching for the scratch on her neck that—okay, *ow*—might be a little more than a scratch.

"I don't care," she said. Dimly, she registered voices, a bunch of shouting and movement she couldn't focus on.

She was too busy realizing she was alive. "You really meant it, when you said you'd do anything to keep me safe."

"Yep. I was a total decoy. But I needed to be sure you were okay before Garza could do his thing."

"Oh," Tara breathed, leaning into Xander's embrace. "Well, yes. I'm very, very okay."

"Nice head butt, by the way," he said, holding her tight.

"Nice rescue," she murmured.

And then everything went dark.

XANDER LOOKED at Tess Riley and frowned. "Are you absolutely *sure* she's okay?"

Dr. Riley gave up a laugh, which would've been a good sign if Tara hadn't nearly fucking died at the hands of a madman mere hours ago. "I know what it's like to have someone you love endure a trauma, so I'll go through it one more time for you, Officer Matthews. Ms. Kingston sustained a blow to the back of the head, right here"—she indicated an X-ray on a large digital monitor in the exam room—"that resulted in a concussion. A subsequent MRI was clear. My very capable resident, Dr. Drake, repaired the laceration on her neck with five stitches. Dr. Drake, by the way, has excellent hands and is on his way to becoming an accomplished surgeon. Just don't tell him I said so. Other than a few mild contusions to her wrists and ankles, Ms. Kingston is just fine. I expect she'll make a full recovery in a few days. Provided she's well cared for, of course."

"I told you," Tara said, eyeing him from the gurney. "I'm fine."

"You're going to *be* fine," Dr. Riley corrected. "But apparently, you've caused quite a ruckus in my waiting room."

"I have?" Tara asked, and shit. Xander hadn't wanted to rile her up, but...

"Yeah. I guess Sansone resisted when the Intelligence Unit tried to take him into custody. They tried to bring him in without a fuss, but he went for one of the guards' guns, and..."

"Detective Hollister tasered him into next week," Dr. Riley said, not unhappily. "Don't worry. We'll get him nice and fixed up so he can stand trial. Between him and the huge dude recovering from a concussion just like yours, I'm sure you'll be busy when you feel up to working again."

"Oh, yeah, no," Tara said. "My boss is going to take this one. I'm officially done with Ricky Sansone *and* his partner."

"I don't blame you," Dr. Riley said. "Well, get some rest. You're welcome to stay here as long as you like, but when you're ready to be released, just let me know. I assume Officer Matthews, here, will be your caretaker?"

"Yes," Xander said without hesitation. "I'll make sure she gets whatever she needs."

"Great. Take your time. Just ring the nurses' station if you need anything."

Xander thanked her quietly before turning to Tara. "You scared the ever-loving shit out of me today, you know."

"I didn't mean to," Tara said, her auburn brows furrowing. "Amour's okay, though, right?"

"She's perfect," he said, because he knew she wouldn't rest until she was absolutely certain Amour was just fine. "After Judge Waters suspended the trial, she went to the Thirty-Third with Isabella. Apparently, Amour is a whiz at picking out a baby registry."

"Seriously?" Tara asked, and Xander raised one hand.

"Scout's honor."

"You're better than a Boy Scout, Xander," she said, her expression growing serious as she reached for his hand. "If you hadn't gotten there when you did—"

"Stop," he said, because seriously, he couldn't bear the thought of *what if*. "I did get there. And you created the perfect opening for me to get you out of there."

"You trusted the Intelligence Unit to have your back," she said, and here, he had to nod.

"You trusted me, and I trust them."

"So, I guess that makes you a good man after all."

"It makes me a man who's falling in love with you."

Xander's face flushed with heat, and okayyyy, guess he was going to say that out loud.

Still, it didn't feel wrong. In fact, the words felt perfect.

So he said them again. "I love you, Tara. I know it sounds a little impulsive and crazy, but I do. I've known it from the minute I saw you, marching toward me at that crime scene with your hands on your hips and all that fire in your eyes. You're smart and fierce and perfect. You stand up for what's right, and I always want to stand beside you. I love you."

"I love you, too," she said, and wait…

"You do?"

"Of course I love you," Tara said with a laugh. "Who else is going to keep me calm when murderous psychopaths try to kill me?"

"You have a point," Xander said. "Although, maybe we could skip the murderous psychopaths from now on, since we've had our fair share?"

"Okay," Tara agreed. "Just as long as there are rubber ducks, I think we'll be just fine."

NOT ready to leave Remington yet? Make sure to preorder the first full-length book in the Intelligence Unit series, "tall, dark, and broody" Detective Matteo Garza's book, THE GUARDIAN, for a special price right here. While you wait for Matteo to steam up your e-reader, you can catch up on the Station Seventeen series right here (Kennedy and Gamble, Isabella, Capelli...they ALL have standalone romances! Follow the link for the first book, or keep reading to see them all in reading order.) And don't forget to subscribe to my newsletter right here for all sorts of exclusives, like freebies and giveaways, sale notices, deleted scenes, new releases, and more!

KIMBERLY'S BOOKS

The Station Seventeen Engine Standalones (super-sexy fire-fighter/cop romantic suspense):

<u>Deep Trouble</u> (Kylie and Devon's story, best friend's little sister/forbidden lovers) (prequel, with 1,001 Dark Nights)

<u>Skin Deep</u> (Kellan and Isabella's book, enemies to lovers)

<u>Deep Check</u> (January and Finn's book, second chance lovers)

<u>Deep Burn</u> (Shae and Capelli's book, opposites attract)

In Too Deep (Luke and Quinn's book, friends to lovers)

Forever Deep (companion novella to Skin Deep, Christmas wedding story)

<u>Down Deep</u> (Kennedy and Gamble's book, forced proximity)

The Remington Medical Contemporary Standalones (sexy medical romance)

<u>Back to You</u> (Charlie and Parker's book, second chance lovers)

<u>Better Than Me</u> (Jonah and Natalie's book, best friends to lovers/accidental roommates)

Between Me & You (Connor and Harlow's book, enemies to lovers)

<u>Beyond Just Us (Tess and Declan's book, marriage of convenience/single parent romance)</u>

<u>Baby, it's Cold Outside (Emmett and Sofia's book, Christmas story/enemies to lovers)</u>

The Cross Creek series (sexy small-town contemporary, available in KU):

<u>Crossing Hearts (second chance lovers)</u>

<u>Crossing the Line (opposites attract)</u>

<u>Crossing Promises (friends to lovers/workplace romance)</u>

<u>Crossing Hope (forbidden lovers)</u>

Read on for a sneak peek at the first book in the Station Seventeen series (yes, Kellan and Isabella's story!), SKIN DEEP.

Kellan made his way up Washington Boulevard, where he'd parked yesterday morning before shift. Funny how quiet the city could be before things like rush hour and regular work-days kicked in, all soft sunlight and clean storefronts. He slid in a breath of cool air, scanning the sidewalk and the two-lane thoroughfare where Station Seventeen was situated.

He saw the woman leaning against his '68 Camaro from forty feet away.

Kellan's pulse flared even though his footsteps never faltered. Long, denim-wrapped legs leading to lean muscles and lush, sexy curves. Loose, confident stance that spoke of both awareness and strength. Long, caramel-colored hair that she tossed away from her face as soon as she saw him coming, and God *dammit*, that was the second time this week he'd been blindsided by Isabella Moreno.

"What are you doing here?" he asked, wincing inwardly as the words crossed his lips. Not that he didn't feel every inch of the attitude behind them, because after her fuck-up had put his sister's life in danger three months ago, he so did. But slapping his emotions on his sleeve wasn't on Kellan's agenda, good, bad, or extremely pissed off. Of course, Isabella already knew he was chock full of the emotion behind door number three, anyway.

She pushed herself off the Camaro's cherry red quarter panel, sliding one hand to her unnervingly voluptuous hip while the other remained wrapped around a cup of coffee. "Waiting for you."

"I got that." His tone left the what-for part of the question hanging between them, and Kellan had to hand it to her. Moreno wasn't the type to mince words.

"I need a favor. I want you to walk me through the scene of Monday's fire."

Jesus, she had a sense of humor. Also, balls the size of Jupiter. "You want me to take you back to the scene of a fire that gutted a three-story house just to give you a play by play?"

She nodded, her brown eyes narrowing against the sunlight just starting to break past the buildings around them. "That about sums it up, yeah."

"It's a little early for you to be punching the clock, isn't it?" he asked. Most people weren't even halfway to the door just shy of oh-seven-hundred on a weekday morning.

Moreno? Not most people, apparently. "What can I say? I'm feeling ambitious."

Kellan resisted the urge to launch a less-than-polite

comment about her work ethic, albeit barely. "I already told you and Sinclair everything I know."

"Okay." Her shoulders rose and fell beneath her dark gray leather jacket, easy and smooth. "So humor me and walk me through it again anyway."

His sixth sense took a jab at his gut, prompting him to give the question in his head a voice. "Is this part of the investigation?"

"Why do you ask?" she said, and yeah, that was a no.

"Because you called it a favor, and you just answered my question with a question."

Moreno paused. "I'm a cop. We do that."

Nope. No way was he buying this. Not even on her best day. "And I'm a firefighter who's not interested in putting his ass in a sling just to humor you with an unsanctioned walk-through."

The RFD might offer a little latitude on firefighters revisiting scenes—a fact Kellan would bet his left nut Moreno damn well knew—but just because he'd worked the job didn't mean he had carte blanche to prance through the place like a fucking show pony now that the fire was out.

Not that a little thing like protocol seemed to bother Isabella in the least. "Your ass will be fine. I'll take full responsibility."

"I'm pretty sure I've heard that one from you before."

The words catapulted out before Kellan could stop them. Moreno flinched, just slightly, but it was enough. "Look, I need to get back onto that scene," she said. "Are you going to help me or not?"

His brain formed the word "no", but all of a sudden, he registered the weary lines bracketing her eyes and the shadows that went with them like a matched set of good and tired, and his mouth tapped into something entirely different. "Did you even sleep last night?"

An image of her in bed, honey-bronze skin against pristine white sheets, barreled through his mind's eye, and Jesus. Maybe he was the one who needed some shuteye if his subconscious was going to go off the deep end like that.

"Not really, no," Isabella said, shifting her weight from one heavily soled boot to the other in order to stand at flawless attention on the sidewalk. "I was a little busy worrying about those girls in the pictures you found."

The answer hit him like the sucker punch it was. Fuck. *Fuck.* "Your boss doesn't seem to find them quite as concerning," Kellan managed, and at her look of surprise, he continued. "If he did, he'd have opened an official investigation and you wouldn't have needed to haul yourself all the way down here at o'dark-thirty to ask me to get you into that house, right?"

For a long minute, she just studied him with those chocolate-brown eyes. But rather than copping to anything, Moreno said, "And what's your gut on those pictures, hmm?"

Damn. For a detective who had botched the hell out of keeping Kylie safe, she sure was asking all the right questions to get him to cave.

Unease tightened his muscles, speeding his heartbeat by just a notch. "I have a sister. What do you think?"

"I think those photos are evidence of a crime being committed against the women in them, and I think you wouldn't have had your captain call them in unless you do, too."

She's kind of got you there, dude. Kellan exhaled, mashing down on his inner voice. "So how come your sergeant doesn't agree?"

"I never said he didn't," Moreno pointed out. Her expression matched the utterly noncommittal tone of her words, but come on. He hadn't just fallen off the turnip truck, for Chrissake. She wouldn't ask him to bring her back to the scene of this fire unless it was her last resort.

Kellan hit her with a high-level frown. "If you want me to consider helping you out here, the least you can do is not bullshit me before I'm caffeinated."

"Fine." She pressed her lips together, a swath of light brown hair serving as cover for her eyes as she lasered her gaze toward the sidewalk beneath her feet. "*Hypothetically*, on occasion we catch cases that don't have quite enough evidence to pursue in an official capacity."

Seriously? "You have pictures," he said. What better evidence was there?

"Yeah, and that's all I have. Pictures of women I can't identify, who might be of legal age and participating in consensual acts."

Kellan's stomach knotted. He was hardly vanilla when it came to sex, but the girls in those photos had looked terrified, not to mention dangerously young. Role play was in a whole different universe than rape. "You don't really think what's going on in those photos is consensual, do you?"

"You don't really think I'd ask you to take me back to the spot where you found them to look for more evidence if I did, do you?" Moreno asked archly, and *damn*, she was tough.

Too bad for her, so was he. "Let me get this straight. You want me to take you back to a house the fire marshal has almost certainly condemned, without the permission or knowledge of your sergeant or my captain, just because you have a gut feeling that can't be substantiated by any evidence found at the scene?"

"Give the firefighter a gold star. That's exactly what I want."

Kellan took it back. Jupiter wasn't big enough for the stones on this woman. "Give me one good reason why I should put my ass on the line for you."

Before he could move or blink or even breathe, Isabella had stepped toward him, so up close and personal that he could feel the warmth of her breath on his face as she said, "Because I don't want you to put your ass on the line for *me* at all. I want you to do it for those women. You and I seem to be the only people who think this case is worth pursuing right now, and I can't change that without more evidence, which I can't get if you don't help me. So are you in or not?"

And don't forget to read this sneak peek of Kennedy and Gamble's book, DOWN DEEP, too!

Ian Gamble was going to get good and fucking drunk. A solid bender wasn't usually in his repertoire, what with the whole twenty-four hours on, forty-eight hours off thing he did at the fire house. By the time he caught up on his sleep and his workouts, there wasn't usually much time to get shit-faced and recover, especially if he was going to abide by Remington Fire Department's eight-hours-from-bottle-to-throttle rule. Being Station Seventeen's engine lieutenant and a former Marine, Gamble was big on regs. Order. Control.

But tonight was an exception. One he made every August. One he'd continue to make until the day he went into the ground.

Because he was the only person left from his recon unit who could.

"Hey, boss! Who died?"

The words, spoken by Gamble's engine-mate and resident smartass, Shae McCullough, ripped into the old scars he kept hidden, turning them fresh and raw. "What?"

She traded a tiny bit of the sparkle in her stare for concern, sliding into the space next to him at The Crooked Angel's bar. There was no way McCullough could know how spot-on her words had been, namely because Gamble had never told another living soul all the gory details (okay, fine...or any details) of his past as a Marine, aside from his CO and the headshrinker they'd made him see after he'd come home from Afghanistan. But he had to give his friend credit. She wasn't an idiot. In fact, right now, she was looking at him shrewdly enough to make his heart pump out a potent cocktail of defenses and dread.

"That's a mighty serious look you're wearing," McCullough said, and yeah, it was time to lock this shit up, no matter how tight the two of them were.

"All good. Just having a drink since we're not on shift tomorrow." Gamble picked up his beer for a nice, long draw as proof, rolling his shoulders beneath his T-shirt and leather jacket combo. "What about you?"

The gruff redirect worked, just as he'd known it would. "I'm watching DC lose her shirt to Faurier," McCullough said brightly.

Shit. "Please tell me that's not literal."

Without waiting for a response, he turned from his spot at the bar to laser a stare at the pool table by The Crooked Angel's side door. Lucy de Costa, who had been nicknamed "DC" by both McCullough and their other engine-mate, Kellan Walker, on her first day in-house a couple of months ago, was standing among the other firefighters from Seventeen and a few cops from the Thirty-Third district, wearing an epic frown and—thankfully—her damned shirt.

McCullough threw her head back and laughed. "Please. Girlfriend might be a rookie, but she's not making *that* rookie mistake. Especially not with a horndog like Faurier."

Gamble exhaled in relief. Not that it was technically any of his business who de Costa got down and dirty with. But she was brand-spanking-new to the RFD, and it was his job to look out for her. Plus, if she decided to ride the bone train with their rescue squad's second-in-command—or any other firefighter at Seventeen, for that matter—it would likely make Gamble's universe a fuck-ton more complicated in terms of getting her *and* her bed-buddy to focus. Especially when shit started burning down.

"I assume you're talking about Lucy," said McCullough's live-in boyfriend and tech brainiac for the police department's elite intelligence unit, James Capelli, as he walked up to stand beside her. Gamble wasn't shocked to see the guy, mostly because he and McCullough were far enough gone for each other to be attached at the hip most of the time, but also because Gamble's head was on a permanent swivel. He'd seen Capelli approaching from fifteen paces out. Not to mention where he, and nearly everyone else in the bar, had been in the room for the last fifteen minutes on top of that. Score one for the highest state of awareness. Not that Gamble could turn that shit off even if he wanted to.

Which he didn't.

"Oh, hey, babe!" McCullough's run-of-the-mill smile became something altogether deeper in less than the span of a heartbeat at the sight of Capelli. "Yeah. She's scrappy, and she talks a good game, but Faurier's kicking her ass pretty good at eight-ball."

"That's definitely accurate on all counts," Capelli agreed. "But as far as her getting too personal with him, I don't think you have anything to worry about. I just overheard her telling Quinn she'd rather be skinned alive with kitchen shears than date a fellow firefighter."

Gamble's brows lifted to match the *huh* winging through his veins, and he slid another glance at the spot where de Costa now stood talking to Station Seventeen's lead paramedic. "I'm assuming that's a direct quote," he said.

Capelli sent an ultra-serious look past his thickly framed glasses. "I have an eidetic memory, Lieutenant. Not to put too fine a point on it, but yes, any time I quote someone, it's exact."

McCullough laughed, clearly used to and enamored with the guy's quirks. "Looks like DC's virtue is safe. Even if her pride isn't," she added. Spinning her gaze back to Gamble, she said, "You coming over for a game? I'm not nearly as bad at eight-ball as de Costa. Bet I could take you."

"Nah. Not tonight."

"You sure?" Surprise mixed with the slight hint of worry on her face. "You've been sitting here by yourself for almost an hour."

Ah, hell. He'd nearly gone to a shitty dive bar instead of their regular hangout for this very reason. Firefighters were a perceptive bunch, their lives depending on it and all. He probably shouldn't be shocked that McCullough had noticed the personal-space bubble he'd created around himself. The two of them were fairly tight, with her having the most tenure on engine besides him. On any other night, he would've taken her up on her challenge, then had to keep every last one of his wits about him to try and beat her. But tonight wasn't any other night. It was the only night out of the year when his fire house family wasn't enough to dull his memories.

Five had gone out. One had come back. The only thing

that could dull the anniversary of that came in a shot glass and clocked in at eighty proof.

"Yeah. I'm sure," Gamble said. "I've got something to take care of over here."

Whether McCullough believed him or had decided to let him off the hook, he couldn't be sure, but either way, she simply shrugged. "Suit yourself, chicken."

"That's Lieutenant Chicken to you," Gamble reminded her.

"Oooh, I kind of like the sound of that." When he skewered her with the most "don't you dare" stare he could work up, she grinned and—smartly—reconsidered. "But maybe I'll stick with good, old-fashioned Gamble, just for the sake of tradition...and not being assigned to scrub the fire house toilets with a toothbrush during next shift."

"You're in love with a smart woman," Gamble told Capelli, who finally allowed a smile to sneak a half-path over his mouth.

"I'm well aware of her aptitude."

"Aw, flattery will get you everywhere, baby," McCullough said with a laugh. She took a step back, letting Capelli thread his arm around her shoulders before turning back to give Gamble one last smile. "You know where we'll be if you change your mind."

Gamble lifted his chin in acknowledgment. "Copy that."

Watching the two of them head back toward the pool table, he couldn't help but shake his head a little at the idea of a relationship that deep. Sexual attraction, he got. A couple of hot-sex hookups here and there to satisfy said attraction? He got those, too. But the sort of no-holds-barred love that McCullough and Capelli and a few other members of Seventeen had tumbled into lately seemed as alien to him as little green men, complete with flying saucers and moon dust.

People swore they saw that shit; hell, they believed it in their bones. But as far as he was concerned, they were all fucking crazy.

"Well, well. Lieutenant Gamble. Aren't you a sight for sore eyes?"

The throaty, feminine voice hit Gamble point-blank from the business end of the bar, and God *damn* it, he must have more of a beer buzz than he'd thought. He was almost always hyper-aware of his surroundings—especially when they involved someone as sexy as Kennedy Matthews. Yet, here she was in front of him, wearing a form-fitting red top and a brash, brows-up stare, and for a fleeting second, he wondered if her smile tasted as tart as it looked.

"If you say so," he told her, while snuffing out the unbidden thought. Not that he hadn't entertained it dozens of times before, or thought about tasting Kennedy in places other than her mouth. But as the manager and head bartender of their regular hangout, she was almost as much a part of his inner circle as his fellow firefighters, and—like his rookie—Gamble knew far better than to muddy that water with a good, fast fuck. "Can I get another beer, please?"

Kennedy's darkly lined eyes widened for just a heartbeat before narrowing over the frost-covered bottle in his hand, the piercing in her eyebrow glinting in the soft overhead light of the bar.

"That one is nearly full."

"Not for long." He was already on his way to a decent beer buzz, courtesy of the bartender who had been working this section of the bar before Kennedy had come out of the back. He'd stick to beer for now to keep a low profile. Once everyone from Seventeen started heading home in a little while, he'd kick his night into high gear.

Kennedy paused. She was tougher than she looked, which was saying something since she had as much ink and even more hardware than Gamble did, with a watercolor tattoo that spanned from the middle of her bicep to her shoulder and the top of her chest, and tiny silver studs and hoops marching all the way up her left ear to match the piercing in her eyebrow. But he returned her calculating stare with one of his own, until she lifted one sleekly muscled shoulder and let it drop.

"It's your liver, tough guy."

She reached into the cooler built in beneath the bar, popping the cap off the beer she'd unearthed and placing it over a napkin on the glossy wood in front of him before turning to saunter off. Gamble watched her go, his eyes lingering on the way her ass filled out her jeans like a fuckable version of an upside-down heart. He couldn't deny being tempted. Shit, he'd have to be pulseless not to be. But even if he *did* decide to break his personal protocol and see if Kennedy was up for blowing off a little steam between the sheets, it wouldn't be tonight.

Tonight wasn't about anything other than him, a bottle of Patrón Platinum, and the ghosts he'd never shake.

ACKNOWLEDGMENTS

Huge, heartfelt thanks go out to my cover dream team—
Christopher John (CJC Photography), who shot a perfect
"Xander" photo of Eric Guilmette, and Shannon Passmore
(Shanoff Designs), who turned it into cover gold. I hope
everyone judges this book by its cover! Nicole Bailey (Proof
Before You Publish), you are a saint for keeping my
grammar in line, my timelines on the straight and narrow,
and my words as they should be.

To Rachel Hamilton and Jen Williams, who beta read even
when things were ugly. Thank you for not letting me end
this book with a tidal wave that engulfs them all, the end.

To my readers—I see you, Taste Testers!—thank you for
wanting more from Remington, and for reading each book
so eagerly every time.

To my family (whether were related or not, you know who
you are), I cannot get through a single day without your
support, hugs, advice, encouragement, more hugs, and wine.

And to D and the girls (yes, Olive, you, too), y'all are my
whole heart. I love you more.

Made in the USA
Monee, IL
19 October 2020